7 Deadly Sins

Sins of Bear Corner
Book 2

By: Mary Reason Theriot

Dedication

Without the love and support of my family and friends, I would not have pursued this new path in life. I would especially like to thank those that have proofread copy after copy, to give me their honest opinion of the books.

Theresa, thank you so much for your continued encouragement. Without you, some of the characters would not have "come to life."

To my wonderful husband Malwen, your continued love and support mean the world to me. I don't know what I would do without you in my life. One of these nights I'm sure you will be able to sleep with both eyes closed. Eventually I should run out of ideas... or maybe not. These books wouldn't be what they are without you pushing me forward.

To Yuri Theriot thank you for helping me with this book. I enjoyed discussing the concept behind the book as well as the seven deadly sins.

To Don Reason and Malcolm "Phil" Theriot for sharing your knowledge and experience of Law Enforcement protocol.

To my fans, I would like to offer a special thank you for your continued support.

ISBN-10: 1-945393-12-2
ISBN-13: 978-1-945393-12-9

Also Available by Mary Reason Theriot:

The Hideaway

The Traveler

Dr. Frankenstein

Above Suspicion

Horror in the Night

Deadly Seduction

Echoes on the Bayou

Coming Soon:

A Kiss So Deadly

A Deadly Combination

www.maryreasontheriot.com

Prologue

He dropped the knife into the sink. This was not just any knife, though. This knife set a soul free earlier in the evening. It was sharp enough to cut through steel. He watched in fascination as the blood of the sinner mixed with the water as he washed his hands. He had completed the first part of God's mission. His mother's soul was one-step closer to gaining entrance into the Kingdom of God. When his mother was diagnosed with cancer, he promised her they would defeat it. Not only had he failed to keep his promise, but he had let her commit the ultimate sin, suicide. The church denied his request to allow her body to pass through because she had committed such a grievous mortal sin.

That night he begged God to help his mother's soul find everlasting peace. There had to be a way for their heavenly Father to forgive his mother! That was when God came to him with a mission, eradicate the sinners and he would allow his mother eternal rest in heaven. Only after these sinners had atoned for their sins would his mother gain entry into His kingdom. Each day that her soul remained confined in purgatory was a day of unrest for him.

Once he finished cleaning his hands, he moved onto the knife. The water in the sink was now a crimson red. He closed his eyes and visualized setting her soul free. He laid the knife on the counter to dry. He would return it to his arsenal of tools after his shower.

He placed his dark clothes in a black plastic trash bag. There was no sense in washing them. When he was preparing to begin God's mission, he purchased several disposable outfits from a thrift store in New Orleans. He knew the importance of disposing of any evidence as soon as he released a soul. He could not take the chance of the police stopping him just yet. First, he must complete his mission so God could forgive his mother and free her soul from Purgatory.

He headed to the bathroom and turned on the shower. Soon steam filled the room. He stepped into the shower and let the hot water run over him. He lathered the soap on his body over and over again until the water ran clear.

He dressed in dark clothes once again. By daybreak, this town would know what happened to sinners.

Chapter 1

Pride

Detective Chad Picou had not once regretted transferring from Baton Rouge, Louisiana to Bear Corner. He had felt welcomed here since the minute he moved into his house. He had never experienced such hospitality. Several of his neighbors even brought over little gift baskets and homemade goodies.

He also found out that he fit right in with the locals. When he moved here, he feared that he would miss the hustle and bustle of the city, but he preferred this small town way of life. He was comfortable in this quaint town and loved the people. Living in Bear Corner had also brought him closer to his Cajun heritage.

His duties as a detective could be almost mundane at times. Nothing much went on in the sleepy town, that was until storm waters revealed Carl Ledet's deadly secret earlier this year. Picou could finally close his eyes and not see Ledet holding that knife to Mia. His blood ran cold at the mere thought of what she had endured at the hands of that man. The only good thing that came from the experience involving Ledet was that it brought them even closer together.

Mia was the best thing that could have ever happened to him. She was the first woman he envisioned himself growing old with, which was why he married her.

Chapter 2

Mia Picou was about to stop for the day when her mom called, "Mia darling, I hate to bother you but I need a favor. I need someone to take your dad to his chiropractor appointment today. I am still at Chris's and it may be a little longer before he is done. He was running late this morning."

"Mom, you know I never have a problem helping out with Dad. I will head over to get him right now."

Samuel Cheramie had been her dad's chiropractor for a little over a year now. He had been a great help to him. Chiropractic treatment may not be an option for every patient with Multiple Sclerosis but it had relieved some of her dad's symptoms, and that was good enough for her. Whatever Samuel did there, her dad moved around better after a few tweaks from him.

Mia still remembered the day her dad came home and told them about his MS diagnosis. Back then, she had no idea what this disease meant, but over the years as she witnessed the MS progress, she had a lot more respect for her dad. He was once a very energetic man that had dealt well with the blows MS sent him. It had been over fifteen years since his diagnosis and in the last two years his walking had become worse. He now relied heavily on his cane, but thanks to Samuel, he had been able to prove the neurologist wrong. His doctor told him that by now he would be in a wheelchair. He was doing everything in his power to stay standing on his own two feet. Thanks to Samuel, it was a very good possibility.

Samuel refused to allow Mia's dad to give up, no matter what. More importantly, he did not take any gruff from her dad. Her dad could be a challenge at times.

The heat of the day hit Mia as soon as she stepped outside. The sky was a brilliant blue without a cloud in sight and there was no breeze blowing, only a wall of humidity that made the day hazy. She could actually see the heat steaming off the roads. If it was this hot now, she dreaded what summer would be like. The weatherman last night had reported there was no rain in the forecast for the next several days. They desperately needed the rain. It was so dry here the ground was cracking.

Walking to her car, she went over some new ideas for her bakery, Mia's. She was thinking of offering a variety of Italian sodas to help people quench their thirst as the summer months heated up. The young and the old flocked indoors, desperately trying to find some relief from the oppressive Louisiana heat. As the morning wore on in the summer, no one would be looking for coffee, but something ice cold. Iced coffees may go over well, but the Italian sodas would be something different here.

After picking up her dad, Mia took him to Samuel's office. She made it there with seconds to spare. "I'm sorry Samuel. Mom is tied up at the moment and I had to finish picking everything up before closing shop."

"That's okay Mia. Will your mom be back to pick up your dad?"

"To be honest, I didn't ask. I just figured I would wait here and work while he was in the exam room."

Her dad looked over at her, "I'm not an invalid! If you need to go do something, I can wait around here for your mother."

Mia shook her head, "That is nonsense Dad. Besides, I can catch up on some work while I wait. Otherwise, it probably won't get done."

Her dad gave her a hard stare, "If you say so, but I don't need a babysitter."

Mia let out a chuckle, trying to put her dad at ease. "Have you ever thought that maybe I do? Besides, I need to make out a grocery list and go over several other things for the bakery."

He gave her a kiss on her cheek, "If you insist. I need to get back there and let this man start cracking these old bones or it will be nightfall by the time I am done."

While her dad was in the back, Mia jotted down a few new recipes she had going through her head along with a list of what she needed to get for the bakery.

After her experience with Carl Ledet, she realized just how short life really was. When Chad Picou asked her to marry him, she was elated with joy. She had dreamed of finding the kind of love her parents had, and she believed she had that with Chad. She was happy with their new life together and wanted to start a family right away.

Before Mia knew it, Samuel was escorting her dad back into the waiting room. She gave him a smile, "It looks like you had a good session today."

Samuel nodded his head, "The old man did well. See you Thursday."

***

He watched as father and daughter left. Why couldn't all families stick together through life's turmoils? Mr. Arnold's diagnosis was a huge blow, and yet his wife and child continued to stick by him. People could learn a lot from the Arnold family.

He had always loved touching people, craving that physical contact. That was why he became a chiropractor. He was able to touch people all day without complaint. He inflicted pain through manipulating uncooperative joints, helping the healing process. No one would ever suspect the real reason he pushed a little too hard, pushing the pain beyond reasonable limits. Pain was good for the spiritual body as well. It cleansed the body and purified the heart.

In his professional life, he displayed a calm, controlled, and passionate concern for his patients. No one knew what he was truly like. He kept everyone at arm's length and always would.

He may be considered an excellent chiropractor here, but he was so much more. He was a healer of the soul as well as the body.

Chapter 3

He enjoyed this part of the ritual. The perilous night gave him such a thrill. His eyes stayed alert with the exhilaration of setting another soul free. Like a hungry animal stalking its prey, he waited for the perfect moment to strike.

He hid in the shadows waiting, the darkness of his car cloaking him. A muscle spasm ran through his legs. He had been sitting in the car longer than he would have liked, and his body was protesting. He had hoped his intense workout from this morning would help him be nimble tonight, but he must have overworked his muscles more than he realized. He believed in keeping his body as fit as his soul. He adjusted his position without making too much movement. He had been waiting for over an hour for her, but he had yet to see her. He did not believe in tardiness, any change in his strict schedule upset him. For a successful plan to work, everything must run like clockwork.

He had been following her for over two weeks now, had studied her routine, observed her activities just like a private investigator. He had to be certain that she needed to confess her sins and repent before he could save her soul. He overheard her talking one day on her phone and realized she was a sinner. She could not stop talking about spending her husband's money. She flashed the ring on her hand to make sure everyone in the waiting room took notice. She was usually such a predictable creature, but she was running late today.

From what he had learned, Victoria Russo was only concerned about one thing, shopping. She spent her days in and out of stores, showing off her purchases at lunch with friends.

Victoria knew her husband had a mistress, but as long as she ignored his indiscretions, he permitted her to spend as much money as she wanted. It was a win win situation for the both of them.

Growing up, she did not concern herself with going to college. She set her eyes on marrying a rich man and living the life of luxury. She played her cards right and so far everything was working out perfectly. She didn't even have to sleep with the man; his mistress took care of his needs.

With tires squealing, he saw her car come zipping into the driveway. He watched her every move as if she was beckoning him to complete his mission and save her soul. She must atone for her sins.

"Perfect," he thought to himself when he saw her pull into the drive. He feared he would have to wait another day before he released her soul. He glanced at his watch and noticed she was over an hour late. He wondered what kept her detained, no matter though, he would complete his mission tonight. As she exited the car, he watched her every move. Soon he would make his move.

His heart pounded violently in his chest. Soon he would set her soul free, cleansing her of her sins. Not many people in town knew of her sins. She easily deceived those who knew her. She was guilty of the mother of all deadly sins. Pride was from which all others were born. Pride was an ego gone wild, a vicious beast. Fate, though, had a way of making things right. He became overwhelmed with a feeling of euphoria that few would ever understand.

He stood in the shadows of the trees outside of her house, waiting to enter. Nightfall brought no relief from the heat wave that plagued the state. His shirt clung to his back, already damp with sweat. The rain started to fall and the wind picked up. He ignored the elements as he was on God's mission, one he must complete.

God sent him to this city of decadence that needed saving. So many people here needed purification of their sins. He had been waiting for so long to do God's will and now the time had come. The people in this town needed to know what happened to sinners. They must repent for their sins and change their ways.

He had dressed in dark clothes to blend into the night. He had situated himself before everyone came home from work. He did not want to be seen driving in the neighborhood.

He watched as the lights in her house went off. He caught a hint of movement in her room. Moving cautiously along the shadows to her back door, he quickly opened it and entered the house. He headed straight to her bedroom.

He could already feel his hands on her body, releasing her. It had been so very easy to break into her house.

***

Victoria Russo hated when her husband was away, even if they didn't sleep in the same room. When he was away, she tended to hear every creak and moan this old house made. As she settled into bed, she stopped suddenly and listened. She thought she heard a creak, as if someone was coming up the stairs. Her heart nearly stopped.

She got out of bed and peered out the window. She was half-afraid she would see something sinister lurking around. "Stop it," she told herself. She was just hearing things. It was the wind. She could see the moss that hung from the massive oak tree swaying in the night.

As she crawled back in bed, she heard the noise again. Her throat went dry. She told herself she was being silly. There was nothing evil in her home. She was letting her imagination work overtime tonight! She turned on the TV to drown out any noise she thought she might have heard. She fell asleep to the sounds of a TV show playing in the background.

She awoke suddenly, unsure of what had startled her and looked around. Before she could react, the intruder was on top of her. He was impossibly strong; his nails dug into her to stop her flailing.

He pulled out the ketamine soaked rag and held it over her mouth and nose. The drug quickly weakened her. The fight to flee left her body. Everything went hazy. Her eyelids were heavy as she succumbed to the drug.

***

An urgency to release her soul plagued him and he rushed home, not paying attention to the speed limit. He reprimanded himself; it would not do his mission any good if they found an unconscious woman in the back of his SUV. That would be difficult to explain.

He pulled down the long narrow road that led to his house. His plantation consisted of several acres with the house overlooking the bayou. When he moved here, he asked the real estate agent to find him a historical home that offered privacy from the town. The pictures were nothing like what he saw, but still if he closed his eyes, he could see the hidden potential in the house.

The first time he drove up to it, he seriously considered backing out of the purchase. It reminded him of a haunted house. Then he walked to the back of the property. When he saw the old smokehouse, he knew God had sent him here. This was where he would carry out God's mission.

Trees dripping with Spanish moss shrouded the old plantation home. Instead of scaring him away, the view from the outside just added to the house's mystique. He had lived here for over a year now and he had yet to renovate the main house. The white paint was peeling in several areas including the enormous white columns that framed the massive house.

When he first saw the structure, it was far larger than he had imagined. A porch wrapped around the ground floor and an enormous balcony encircled the second story. There were arch shaped French doors for the windows, confirming the magnificence of the once beautiful and graceful plantation. When you stepped into the house, the old wooden plank floors had a tendency to creak and pop, echoing through the house.

The old plantation had been up for sale for ten years before he purchased it. No one dared to take on the monstrosity and expense of fixing it up. He had a feeling the house was just waiting for him though. It knew of God's mission for him. It was the perfect place to save these souls.

The former residents even left the antique furniture when they moved. When he first walked through the door, it reminded him of an ancient tomb. Heavy layers of dust coated the surfaces of everything it touched. After removing the layers of grime, he found that the hearths had very detailed marble mantels and beautiful woodwork. Someone took a lot of pride in building this home.

He had gotten the house for a steal knowing when it was fully restored it would go for a lot more. He was busy with his work and God's mission right now though. He had yet to dedicate any time to the house.

He pulled up and brought the sinner to the old smokehouse. This was where he released their souls. Tonight blood would flow in order for her to find salvation.

A heavy fog hovered over the bayou. A smoky mist made its way to the house. The damp air was a perfect marriage of the murky bayou water and the fragrances of confederate jasmine and gardenia. He listened to the creatures of the night scurry about. It was the perfect evening for atonement.

He placed her bound and gagged body into the chair, moving quickly to secure her. He noticed how beautiful this sinner was. Even in her state of distress, she was a temptress. His crotch tightened. He chastised himself. He was on God's mission and must avoid the temptation of this seductress. She was vile, evil. He could not think of her as a woman, but as a sinner. She had committed one of the deadliest of sins. She was full of pride and must repent.

* * *

Why was he doing this to her? Surely someone as good looking as him did not need to force himself on a woman. He had an athletic body, square jaw and a straight nose. He had a movie star quality about him until you looked into his eyes. There was no life in them. You could see the evil in his eyes. He was eerily cold and emotionless.

She began to cry, trying to erase the images of things he could do to her from her mind. No matter how hard she tried, she could not stop the visions from running through her mind. Her blood began to curdle. She feared her captor was cold-blooded and unmercifully cruel.

"Are you ready? Are you prepared to atone for your sins?" She looked into his eyes and saw blackness; they were devoid of life. She let out a whimper. "Do you accept Jesus as your Lord and Savior?"

She nodded her head to acknowledge she did. She was not ready to die. She tried to break free from her restraints, but the duct tape refused to give way. She tried to talk, but the gag only muffled her sounds.

Her captor bent down to touch her and she flinched. He glared at her, "I need to remove the gag so you can confess to your sins." As he removed it, she gasped for air.

"Why are you doing this to me?" she asked.

"It is time for you to pay for your sins."

"What sins have I committed? You know me, I have done nothing wrong."

He grabbed her face and made her look him in the eyes, "You do not give yourself to your husband. You ignore his indiscretions so that you can have money to go shopping. You pride yourself on your worldly goods, but do not care for your husband."

She watched as he wheeled over a cart with various instruments on it. Fear crawled up her skin. She swallowed hard, "What are you going to do to me?"

She wondered what kind of maniac this man was. Was he a religious nut of some sort? The way he leered at her body gave her the creeps.

He ripped open her nightgown. Looking over the tools he had arranged on the cart, he picked up the filet knife. He made a long incision down her torso. She cried as the white-hot pain from the cut seared through her body.

Excruciating, throbbing pain gripped her body. She trembled as he slashed her body repeatedly throughout the night. It was becoming difficult to breathe as the knife continuously invaded her body. She wished this pain would end. Her killer was unmerciful.

She could feel the strength leave her body. She was not ready to die. She tried to beg him not to kill her, to stop but she could not seem to move her mouth.

She had hoped to die peacefully in her sleep at an old age. Never had she imagined it would be like this. She felt cheated. How could God let someone do this to another human being? Especially one that said he was doing this in His name.

She had always taken pride in her body. She could catch any man's attention. She shivered in disgust at how everyone would remember her body. She would become a statistic, a murder victim. Would someone find her body or would he just dispose of her like yesterday's trash? Would her husband mourn her death or would he invite his mistress into their house before he buried her?

Her guttural screams pierced the night. The darkness swallowed them for no one to hear.

She prayed for a means to escape or a savior, someone to rescue her before she was violently murdered. Instead, she endured more pain. He looked down at her. She was near death, ready to be free of this pain. The decision of when to liberate her was his mission. She must atone for her sins to find salvation.

Pools of blood from her injuries grew larger on the floor. Her life slowly ebbed from her body.

***

He watched as the blood flowed from her body. He took the knife and slashed her body, leaving no part of it unmarred by the knife. He made sure to mutilate the perfect body she took pride in.

Euphoria washed over him as he watched rivulets of spilled blood pool on the ground. Picking up his Bible, he found a passage to read over her body. Just saying the words sent a chill along his spine. *Sinners such as her have no place among the just.*

Once he completed this part of his mission, he recited as God instructed, "Dominus vobiscum." His blood sang at the thought of her soul being set free. Slowly he ran his thumb over her forehead, chin, and chest in the sign of the cross. He gave her absolution.

There were still more tasks to be performed before sunrise. He wanted to move her body before rigor mortis set in. He would be able to savor this feeling tonight, once his day was over.

As he displayed her body, he wondered if they would understand the importance of his work. Walking away from the body, his eyes were bright with the tears of joy. He was one-step closer to freeing his mother's soul from purgatory.

Chapter 4

Chad Picou reached across the bed to slap the snooze button on his alarm clock until he realized it was his phone and not the clock grabbing his attention. Damn, he overslept. Mia must have forgotten to reset the alarm clock when she left this morning.

As much as he loved that woman, he did not intend to get up as early as she did. By five o'clock in the morning, she was already hard at work at the bakery. Unlike him, though, she was done and home by four o'clock in the afternoon.

Unfortunately, they only saw each other in the middle of the night, but it worked for them. They also spent time with one another at lunch and most mornings he stopped by her bakery to grab breakfast and a quick kiss before heading off to work.

Picou had been a cop here in Bear Corner for over two years now. Early morning calls have never been good news, especially when they were from the dispatcher, "Picou."

The dispatcher informed him, "Detective Picou, Sheriff Riley asked that I call you. A dead body has been found at the park."

The sleep cleared his mind as soon as he heard the news. "And I'm taking it since you are calling, there is foul play involved."

"Yes, sir. From what I understand, it is bad too. I was told there is no other way to say it except that this was done by a monster."

"Tell the officers working the scene to be careful where they walk. I don't need them traipsing all over the evidence."

"I don't think you have to worry about that sir. It is raining out. Crime scene techs are trying to get what evidence they can before it washes away."

Damn! There went his morning. His adrenaline kicked in, working faster than Mia's coffee. He jumped in the shower, brushed his teeth, combed his hair, and dressed in a blur. He was out the door in less than fifteen minutes.

Detective Chad Picou guided his Dodge Charger along the meandering roadway that led to the park. This was one of his favorite parts of the town. There were massive ancient oak trees with gnarled branches dripping with Spanish moss. The bayou curved around the outskirts of the park like a snake.

He parked the police cruiser alongside the crime scene tape that cordoned off the scene. Patrol cars with flashing blue lights lined the area. He despised the rain, but he hated dealing with murder investigations more.

He tried to brush the drops of rain from his eyes as he approached the crime scene. A maintenance man found the remains of a woman. The heat of the morning was already causing the rainwater to steam as soon as it hit the ground. It would be one hell of a day.

He noticed despite the weather that a crowd was forming. People were starting to gather, curious as to what happened. As with most small towns, word spread like wildfire. A good bit of Bear Corner's citizens craned their necks to catch a glimpse of what was going on in the park. They all knew about the discovery of the body and must be wondering who it was. It was human nature to be curious after all. Everyone would want to know what happened.

Detective Picou scanned the crowd to see who was here. He wondered if one of these fine upstanding citizens was the killer.

The crime scene was buzzing with cops and techs trying to beat the rain. He noticed that the coroner's van had already arrived.

He winced at the expression of dread on the face of the young cop guarding the area. Picou asked, "I take it you were first on scene?"

"Yes, sir."

"Is this your first homicide?"

The young officer nodded, "I feel like I am caught in the middle of a really bad slasher film."

"If you need help with crowd control call someone in. We need to try and send these folks home."

"Yes, sir. Sheriff Riley has some officers heading this way."

He heard Bill Collins from The Tribune call his name, "Detective Picou, do you have any idea whose body has been found?"

Of all the stupid questions, "I just got here Bill. You probably know more than me right now."

The scent of death hung heavy in the air despite the rain. The smell assaulted his senses. He approached Dr. Harrison, the city's medical examiner. He was hunched over what remained of the victim. A crime scene tech was busy photographing the body and surrounding area.

"What do we have doc?" asked Detective Picou.

"You got yourself a vicious killer. The body has practically been cut to pieces."

The remains of the woman lay sprawled near one of the large oak trees in the park. The sight of the corpse disgusted Picou. She was propped against the tree like a rag doll. This crime was particularly heinous, its perpetrator barbaric. What drove someone to commit such an atrocity?

The killer must have taken his time to stage the body. He had a feeling they were going to be dealing with a serial killer. Although, he did not want to breathe a word of that possibility to anyone just yet. What may be worse though was that it looked like they may be searching for a highly organized killer.

Organized killers tended to have a mission or plan in mind when they began killing. They had a place where they preferred to kill with a different disposal site. These killers never acted on opportunity or impulse. Organized killers stalked their victims beforehand and never left the scenes in a frenzy.

This type of killer took their time with the body and scene to ensure they left no evidence behind. They did not like to hide their work and proudly displayed their kills, but would take great measures to keep their identity undiscoverable.

This killer had a specific message he wanted to convey, and it was their job to figure out what that was. An extreme amount of rage showed on the victim. It was up to them to figure out if this person represented a great personal significance to their killer.

"What do you make of the body, doc?"

"Completely brutal. I will go over the body with a fine tooth comb to see if maybe our killer cut himself in the process."

Detective Picou agreed. His partner, Detective Jo Melancon, looked up at the sky, "This rain doesn't help much either."

Looking at the corpse something caught his eye, "There is something underneath her." He took his gloved hand and gently pulled out the piece of paper. "It appears our unsub left us a note."

Picou read the note, "Victoria Russo must repent for her PRIDE."

"Looks like our killer wanted to let us know who the victim was and why he killed her," stated Melancon.

Dr. Harrison asked, "Do you think there will be another murder like this? The note is probably a message, right?"

Picou ran his hands through his hair, "I hate to speculate right now and start rumors running rampant, but I think you are correct. I have a feeling that this will not be our only murder."

Melancon agreed, "Not only that, but I have a feeling our perpetrator will only get better at killing. We could be dealing with an organized serial killer who appears to be very attentive. He will pay particular attention to details. He will strive to make each subsequent kill better than the last. I look for him only to leave clues that he wants us to find, such as the note, and nothing else. We don't want to let the public know about our suspicions. It will cause a mass panic."

Picou observed the growing crowd, "The press is going to eat this up."

Melancon agreed, "They are the last ones we want to find out about our suspicions. They are anxious to get a close look at the body. We don't need them to learn about the note the killer left behind. They will bring in the serial killer angle with that little fact."

Picou asked Melancon, "Is the maintenance man still here?"

"He is sitting in his truck. I asked him to wait until the scene was processed before leaving in case we have any questions for him."

Picou walked over to the truck with Melancon, "You found the body?"

"Yes, sir, I was coming to check the trash cans and saw something propped up against the tree. I wasn't sure what it was and went to check it out. I have never seen anything like that before. Who would do that to someone?"

"Did you touch the body?"

"No, sir. I did not even get close to it. I called 911 and sat at the table nearby so I could keep anyone else that may come by away. I didn't think anyone else needed to see that."

Melancon asked, "When you got here, did you see anyone else around?"

The maintenance worker ruefully shook his head, "The park was empty. People usually wait until mid-morning to head this way. You mainly get your lunch crowd during the week. They stop to eat their lunches and stuff. Some moms bring their kids to play on the swings and slides, but it is usually after school when it gets busy. That's why I check trash in the mornings, there are fewer people and I can clean up quickly."

"Have you seen anyone new hanging out around here, maybe checking out the area?"

"Not that I can recall. This is a small town, and just about all the locals hang out here sometime during the day. The kids like to come here and unwind after school before heading home to do their homework during the week. On the weekends, they come to play and get out of the house. A lot of people come at lunchtime to eat and just talk. Parents meet and talk here while their kids play in the afternoons. This is just a typical small town park. I do not know what will happen when they hear about the body. I have a feeling it will be empty for a while."

Picou looked at the poor man, "Why don't you go on home. If you think of anything else just call or stop by the station."

"I'm going back to the maintenance shed. Have to let my supervisor know what happened. I didn't think to call him. He'll probably flip his lid."

Melancon watched as the crowd grew, "This is not what we need right after Carl Ledet. I think half the town is out here now."

Picou looked over at the crowd, "Hopefully, they will head to work or back home soon. Surely they have something better to do than stand out in this weather waiting to hear who is dead."

Melancon shook her head, "Maybe they'll get tired of waiting and leave." Even as she said the words, she did not even believe them. Everyone was still too shaken up from the evil that Carl Ledet did in this town to ignore the discovery of another body.

Sheriff Riley walked over to the two detectives, "If the crowd is bothering you I can have Officer Williams run them off."

Picou shook his head, "Let's hold off Sheriff. I have Officer Zeringue taking pictures of the crowd along with the crime scene. That way we can see if there is anyone paying particular attention or maybe someone new in town that no one seems to know. Besides, if we run them off now they will just think we are trying to hide something."

Sheriff Riley read the note left on the body, "You don't believe that this is someone trying to finish Carl Ledet's work do you? He had told Mia that he killed sinners who needed saving."

Picou let out an exasperated sigh, "I sure as hell hope not. The last thing we need is another religious fanatic going around killing people."

Picou knew that Sheriff Riley had complete faith in both of the detectives' abilities. He had no reason to doubt that they couldn't handle this case. He had come to rely on Picou's knowledge and judgment heavily. Picou was a cracker-jack detective. Melancon was just as good of a detective as he was, though.

Several hours later, they walked into the precinct. They had been at the crime scene for half the day. Walking into the station, he smelled the harsh cleaners the janitors used recently. They would be better off repainting the walls than trying to cover the smell of stale smoke and old coffee that lingered in the building for decades. Even though it was now smoke-free, at one time it housed chain smokers that worked diligently on their assigned cases. Times had changed, though, and now you had to step away from the building to smoke. The cigarette smell still saturated the walls and the tile floor.

***

By the time they made it back to the precinct, they had an hour before the autopsy would begin. Autopsies were an integral part of an investigation. Detective Jo Melancon loathed this part. She did not have a stomach for blood. She could not even watch a medical show on television.

The medical examiner's office was located in a small building just off the hospital. At one time, it was a small office beside the morgue, but as crime increased, a need for a bigger office was recognized and so it was moved. The coroner's office operated under parish jurisdiction, but still provided services to the sheriff's department.

Detective Picou offered to drive over to the ME's office, which was fine with Jo. He pulled the Dodge Charger into the empty parking lot. She watched as he polished off the last of his hamburger. "I don't see how you can eat right before an autopsy."

He shook his head, "It's no big deal. Besides, I was starving." He looked down at her untouched meal, "You didn't even try to eat."

"Why? So I can toss it back up as soon as I walk in the door."

"Stop being such a pussy. Oh wait, you are one." She laughed at his remark. Their work relationship was one where his comments didn't bother her. She had learned this was his personality, and there was no changing him. She wondered how Mia put up with him day in and day out.

Melancon had worked in a male dominated world for a while now. Most of these men were crude, outspoken, and self-absorbed. They believed women did not belong on the force and had few reservations in exhibiting their chauvinism. Over the years, she learned how to survive among them. She brushed off the comments, laughed at their obscene jokes and indecent proposals, more importantly massaged their egos. Sticks and stones may break your bones, but words would never hurt you played in her head more than she cared to admit.

The one rule she had stuck to over the years was never to get romantically involved with a fellow detective, or police officer for that matter.

She was grateful her partner never treated her with the same indifference as her other fellow officers. As partners, somehow they were able to work together perfectly without sexism and have even developed a meaningful kinship. Their working relationship had thrived because traditional terms did not define it. Mutual respect between the two of them had created a strong foundation on which to build a solid friendship. Neither had shown any romantic interest in the other. Besides, Chad was head over heels in love with Mia.

Chapter 5

Bear Corner, Louisiana was a rapidly growing town. The main livelihood of the residents here was still shrimping and working offshore on the oil rigs. Most of the men here tended to do both. What with the economy the way it was and shrimp prices dropping, most shrimpers worked on the rigs and then spent their two weeks off crabbing, shrimping, and fishing depending on the season.

Bear Corner boasted some of the best fishing around. A long wooden dock reached out just over one hundred yards into the Gulf of Mexico. Detective Picou considered this to be one of the most relaxing parts of town. He loved fishing from the pier. The silence and its natural coastal beauty drew him in. Before him was the tranquility of the water and behind him a killer was on the prowl.

He heard his partner walking up behind him. There was no doubt Detective Melancon was a looker. She stood at five feet ten inches with a beauty that would rival any model. She carried her statuesque body with confidence, using her physical charisma to her advantage.

Her curvaceous body often distracted the suspects she interrogated. She was a Louisiana girl, born and raised. When he had transferred here from Baton Rouge, Louisiana, he had been surprised to meet his new partner. He could see that she was gorgeous, but he soon learned that she was also smart. In his opinion, she should have been born a red head; she had a fiery quick temper.

***

Detective Jo Melancon knew from an early age she wanted to be a police officer. It was in her blood; her grandfather had been a cop. Her dad may be a shrimper by trade, but he was also a volunteer firefighter. Maybe it was something in the Melancon blood that wanted them to be a hero. By the age of ten, she had her life planned out. Even though it may not be going as planned, she believed she was helping to make a difference here.

She received a full scholarship from Louisiana State University and graduated with a 4.0 grade point average. She completed her degree in criminal behavior with a background in forensic psychology and profiling methodology. Upon graduation, she entered the Police Academy. Her first assignment was as a patrol officer. She hated it and could not wait to make rank.

She decided to further her education by taking several more online college courses that focused on profiling methodology, criminal behavior, and forensic psychology. Once the sheriff noticed that she was striving to better herself, he took her seriously and not as just another pretty face. She moved up the ranks and had been a homicide detective for almost three years now.

She was the only woman to reach the rank of detective in Homicide, or the police force for that matter. With promotion being limited here in Bear Corner, competition was fierce and when you added in the sexism, it surprised her that she was promoted at all. However, she aced her test, proving that her knowledge of the law, procedures, and investigation process was above par. Following the written exam was the board interview. She sat in front of a bunch of retired and senior detectives where they bombarded her with various questions and scenarios. She excelled in this area, showing them that she could work well under pressure.

Even though she was the only woman here, she refused to hide her femininity. She enjoyed dressing like a woman. She even enjoyed the looks she received from men in general. She would not hide who she was. She had no desire to be one of the boys. All she wanted was to be treated as an equal.

Walking outside to find her partner, she was amazed how life seemed to go on even in the midst of a grisly murder. For a small town, it was extremely busy. The town square was more active than usual. There were at least three school fundraisers going on, including two car washes and a bake sale. The local Knights of Columbus chapter was also having their annual BBQ chicken dinner fundraiser. It seemed as if everyone was doing well. The lines appeared to be long. People were laughing and cutting up as they waited their turn.

Several people were braving the heat of the day and having picnics. In one of the gazebos, someone was boiling seafood. Just smelling the spices made her mouth water. She wondered if it was shrimp or crab, maybe even both. Zydeco music filled the air from a portable radio. She wished she had time to linger.

There were kids running and laughing, waving charred hot dogs in the air. Toddlers ran around barefoot and in diapers, enjoying the feel of the grass on their toes.

Mothers were shouting at their children to stay away from the road.

Unable to stop herself, she eavesdropped on some of the conversations going on around her, wanting to know if the recent murder was on everyone's tongues. So far, there was nothing out of the ordinary. All around her, she saw calm faces and innocuous talk.

From what she heard, it did not sound as if anyone was talking about the brutal murder. She saw the newspaper vendor putting the daily paper in the machine. Peeking to see what the front page looked like she knew the chatter around town would soon be changing. The headline story was about the discovery of Victoria Russo's body. Thankfully, her name was missing from the article, but everyone knew whose body was found today.

They had killings here before, but the murders screamed malicious intent. It appeared that Carl Ledet had cursed this town. Now every time she looked at one of these fine, upstanding citizens, she wondered what they were hiding. What nasty secrets were about to come spilling out as if a dam cracked wide open.

She found Picou not far from the town square. Detective Melancon informed her partner, "The victim's husband is at the precinct."

Chapter 6

A somber silence filled the conference room as they waited for the husband to pull himself together. "We are so sorry for your loss, sir."

"Who did this to her? She didn't have an enemy in the world." His hands were trembling, and his face was white as a ghost.

Mr. Russo had been out of town last night and when he came home, he found his house in disarray. He called 911 as soon as he discovered the mess and his missing wife. Forensics was over at the Russo house searching for evidence as they spoke.

"I keep thinking if only I had come home last night then she would still be alive."

Detective Picou asked, "Mr. Russo, who knew you were out of town last night."

He let out a breath of air, "All of our friends, my secretary, my business partner and I'm not sure who else."

Detective Picou told him, "What happened to your wife is not your fault. Something ugly intervened in her life." He looked upon the distraught man with sympathy.

"Mr. Russo there are some personal questions that I have to ask you."

"I understand, Detective."

"Were you and your wife having marital problems, sir?"

"No, our marriage was fine."

"Did you suspect your wife of having an affair?"

"No, absolutely not. Our marriage may not have been perfect, but after twenty years, I doubt anybody's is. There is no way my wife was having an affair; she did not like to have sex. I am the one having an affair. As long as I supplied my wife with unlimited funds, she overlooked my indiscretions. To be honest with you, I think she was more than happy to have someone else tend to my sexual desires."

By this time, Mr. Russo's eyes had filled with tears. Detective Picou reached out and placed a hand on the grieving man's shoulder. "I'm sorry to ask these questions. You should not blame yourself for what happened to your wife. I wish I could change what she went through, but I promise you this—I will do my best to catch this man."

Chapter 7

Detective Jo Melancon sat at her desk and finished writing her report on Victoria Russo's homicide. At least she could incorporate her notes from her tablet to the computer, making the process easier. As she reviewed the report, the details of the horrific murder played out in her mind one more time.

There was no sexual assault and no apparent robbery. Her purse and phone were still in her house. She had over one thousand dollars in cash in her wallet along with numerous credit cards. She wore a four-carat diamond wedding band, which was still on her body. The killer had one thing on his mind, and that was to torture her. They had no suspects.

Melancon and Picou had spent the day interviewing the victim's husband along with neighbors and friends. She hated telling a loved one about an unexpected death. Unfortunately, no answers were unearthed as to who would want to kill Victoria Russo in such a gruesome manner.

Now she was tired, on edge and had a headache that was almost blinding her. She felt as if her head would split open at any minute. She grabbed her keys and purse before heading out. Her nerves were on edge from this case. The Louisiana sky greeted her as soon as she walked out of the sheriff's office. The blue sky was changing to breathtaking hues of oranges and pinks as the sun set. Until they solved this case, though, she would be missing quite a few sunsets. It would be dark by the time she left in the days to come.

Downtown was still buzzing with activity. You would never know that a murder took place here. After Carl Ledet and then the discovery of the latest body, she figured people would be too nervous to leave their homes, but instead there were people outside enjoying the sunshine. Perhaps most people in town believed that nothing bad would ever happen to them.

Before heading home, she walked over to Chennault's Pharmacy. Étienne Chennault's family had owned the pharmacy ever since she could remember. Étienne took over after his dad retired. Their family came from old money and were one of the richest here in town. However, you would not know it. They were some of the most down to earth people you would ever meet. She would love to live at the Chennault Plantation home, but the latest rumors were that it was falling into disrepair. That was a shame because at one time it was a majestic plantation. She and Étienne had tried dating at one time, but they realized they were better at being friends than romantically involved.

Jo could remember walking in here with her Papa on Saturday mornings peeking over the counter at the candy in the different jars. She especially loved when her Papa gave her a nickel for the gum machine. Thinking back to those days made her miss him even more. It had been almost ten years since cancer took him from them, but walking in here always felt as if he was right beside her.

Even now, the various old-fashioned candy jars still sat behind the counter. Étienne saw Jo walking to the counter, "I understand you had a rough day?"

Jo nodded her head, "It's been one heck of a day that's for sure. I have a splitting headache, and I won't make it home without something."

"You want me to fill one of your prescription migraine meds?"

Jo shook her head, "No, I'm just going to get something over the counter. I have too much going on to sleep for three days right now."

Jo noticed Bill Collins walk in the door and slink over a few aisles behind her. If he were not a journalist, she might actually find herself attracted to him. He was extremely handsome. She watched as he moved around the store. There was a confidence about him.

Jo suspected he was listening to their conversation. She walked over to him and gazed at him for several seconds before saying anything, "Mr. Collins did you want to join in our conversation?"

Bill met her stare and looked deeply into her coffee colored eyes as they narrowed. "I was just curious as to what y'all may be talking about. I'm not stalking you I swear."

Being this close to him, his very scent overwhelmed her. There was a hint of sandalwood mixed with tobacco and possibly honey. It was incredibly sensual.

Detective Melancon continued looking at Bill. She knew the whole town was interested in this murder, and she could not blame him for trying to eavesdrop. He was like the rest of those in here attempting to probe her for answers on the recent killing.

Bill broke the silence, "Would you like to make a comment on the recent murder?"

Jo looked at him and smiled, "Now, Mr. Collins, you know better than that. I'll see you around town."

On her way home, Jo thought about how attractive Bill was. She wondered what it would be like to date him. He seemed so passionate about his work. Would he be as attentive with his girlfriend as he was to his job, or would he be like her and put work first? None of her relationships lasted long. Men did not like when she paid more attention to her job than them. If only she could have a relationship like Chad and Mia. They both had crazy jobs yet they made it work.

Jo reassured herself that she did not need a man, especially with this murder investigation looming over them. She shook herself out of her reverie.

As she passed by Cherie's, located on the bayou, she noticed how busy the bar was tonight. The parking lot and dock were full. Even though the sun had just gone down, everyone wanted to gather and talk about the latest gossip over cold beer, good food, and music. There were probably several Bourree games being played as they drank and talked about everything that happened today. She was tempted to pull into the already overflowing parking lot, but her headache was still lingering. She could picture Pierre on the porch out back cooking a jambalaya or gumbo in his big black pot for tonight's crowd. She could almost taste his chicken and sausage gumbo right now with a big hunk of French bread made by Marie, Pierre's wife. Everyone in town swore that Pierre's gumbo was the best around. Her stomach growled at the thought of food. She should have stopped and picked up supper on her way home. She was too busy to stop and eat anything today. Noise poured out of the building as she passed. The sound of laughter mixed with the Cajun band playing live tonight.

The patrons at Cherie's loved their card playing, drinking and loud music at night, but especially on Friday nights. Sundays were for church and then football. Cherie's catered to a diverse group of people, from roughnecks to fishermen. Occasionally, some of the river rats drifted in, but Pierre was good at keeping the riffraff out of trouble. Being a burly man, he kept even the toughest of men looking for trouble in fear. Cherie's kept the sheriff's office busy on Friday and Saturday nights in this town. By Sunday, the holding cell would be full of drunks who were belligerent and refused an escort home.

Chapter 8

As soon as Mia arrived home, she unloaded her groceries on the kitchen cabinet. Figuring Chad would be home late for supper tonight she cooked a beef roast. She arranged fingerling potatoes, baby carrots, and pearl onions around the pot roast, secured the lid and slipped the roasting pan in the oven. She set the oven to 325 degrees so that it could cook low and slow for the rest of the afternoon. By the time Chad came home, the aroma would be permeating throughout the house.

Later that night, Mia heard Chad opening the front door and ran into his arms. She could tell he had had a bad day and wanted to take his mind off work. She welcomed him home with a warm kiss.

"Mmmm," he whispered in her ear, "I should come home late every night."

She let out a soft giggle, "I thought you might need a warm welcoming after such a hard day."

"This is what I needed after a day like today. Tomorrow won't be any better I'm afraid."

She took his lips in hers and kissed him one more time, "My poor baby."

He wrapped her in his arms, "You are the only thing I need to take my mind off work."

She looked up at him with desire in her eyes, "I have supper cooked if you are hungry."

He pulled her towards the bedroom, "Supper can wait. I want dessert first."

They removed their clothes as they rushed towards the bedroom. She fell onto the bed, locked in his arms. His mouth closed around one of her nipples and his teeth gently scraped over the sensitive flesh. She gasped in delight. He teased the point of her nipple with his tongue, swirling it while tugging on it with his lips. Her back arched to make contact with him. She tingled in anticipation of his touch.

His hands wandered down her body, massaging and kneading as they made their way down. Where his lips and tongue touched, she felt sheer agony. He teased her with light butterfly kisses. His tongue teased her in pure torture. She squirmed, needing more of him. He thrust his tongue deep inside of her. Her hips lifted off the bed in pleasure. Hot kisses made their way up to her breasts one more time, suckling and teasing. He inserted a finger deep inside of her, curling it upward until he found the right spot. She moaned in pure delight.

Chad brought her to the very edge of another orgasm. He teased her with the tip of his erection until neither could stand it anymore. Her whole body cried out when he entered her. He thrust long and hard into her. He rode her hard as orgasm after orgasm ran through her body.

Chapter 9

When he walked into the dark church, it was devoid of life. He was glad they still kept the old church unlocked. So many had gone to locking their doors, but churches should remain open. They should always be open for the needy, for the reverent and the troubled. People should always have a chance to be near God.

He lit two candles. One for his mother's soul and one for the soul he saved. He dropped to his knees by the candles and prayed, prayed desperately for his mother's tortured soul, for the soul he saved and for the souls he was going to save. At first, it had bothered him that he would be taking a life, but he found comfort knowing that this was at God's request. God called him for this mission. He should be overjoyed that he was the chosen one. Not everyone had the chance to perform such a mission for God.

Completing this mission may be the only way for his mother's soul to enter God's Kingdom. He loved her too much to let her spend eternity in purgatory all because she could not take the excruciating pain that plagued her body from cancer. If only she had told him, but she did not want to burden him or his dad with her pain. She died in the middle of the night with no one around her. The hurt of her death had been too much for him and his dad. They were both lost without her. At first, he did not know which way to turn after the church refused to allow her body to pass through its sacred doors. Relief washed over him when God came to him with the answer. He would do anything to keep his mother from suffering in death just as she suffered in the last days of her life.

He wondered if the world would look at him like a monster if they knew. Would they understand his mission? Would his coworkers scorn or detest him for what he had done or would they praise him?

He wished he could talk to someone about his calling. There was no one though, no one he could trust. He doubted anyone would believe him if he told them God had chosen him for this mission. They would not understand why he wanted, no needed, to save his mother's poor tortured soul. Whenever he closed his eyes, he saw the pain still etched on her face. She should be up in heaven, smiling down on him. Instead, she remained trapped in purgatory. She could no longer laugh at his jokes. She was alone in the dark, waiting with other tormented souls. Saving these sinners was the only way God would forgive his mother for her mortal sin. He looked forward to the completion of this mission when his mother would experience sweet relief.

The smell of the votive candles and incense lingered in the sanctuary, the soothing candlelight, and the peacefulness of the church helped ease his spirit tonight. It was time to set another soul free. He felt a rush to complete his mission, to free his beloved mother.

There was one man whose greed consumed him, and everyone knew it. He did nothing to hide the fact that greed was what made his life go round. He cared not who he hurt in the process. He sold his soul to the devil all for money. It was time that he atoned for his sins. Only then would God forgive him for the sins he had committed. He would be one-step closer to completing his duty once he cleansed this soul.

Lowering his head, he prayed even more fervently. He prayed to God for the strength to complete his next assignment. This man kept his house well guarded against those he worried would steal his wealth from him as he had done so many times in the past to others. There were sure to be trials and tribulations before him with this next soul that needed cleansing. However, he had a plan. A greedy man would never turn down a fine gift. Mais non, he would also never share.

Chapter 10

Detective Melancon could not help herself. The next morning she picked up a copy of The Tribune to see what Bill Collins had reported in the paper. She had to admit the man's writing was captivating. Now she knew why the paper bent over backwards for him. His writing seemed to draw you in.

She wondered though how he managed to write about some of the details in the case. He stated several facts that she knew the public were not privy to. That may be something they needed to follow up on. She did not see someone at the sheriff's office releasing information to the press, but there was always a chance that someone had a big mouth.

When she arrived at the sheriff's department, she noticed that the horrendous nature of this crime had put the political machinery of this small town into motion. The Sheriff and the mayor were waiting for Detectives Picou and Melancon to arrive. They both wanted a suspect, and they wanted one now. Mayor Daigle was worried that the newspapers would crucify them for not having answers, stating that the police around here were inept.

Detective Melancon commented, "Maybe we should make an arrangement with The Tribune and the Sheriff's Office. It would need to be a win win situation if we want this to work. This alliance may help us avoid public panic that the media can bring to the case."

She could see the wheels in Mayor Daigle's mind turning. He looked over at Sheriff Riley, "Do you think this is something that may work?"

Picou spoke up, "It sure in the hell can't hurt. How did he get some of those facts anyhow? I would hate to think that we have a leak here in the office."

Sheriff Riley ran his hand over his chin, "I agree with the detectives, sir. It won't hurt the investigation. In fact, it may help us contain what information is released to the press. If more than what we report gets printed, then we definitely have a leak, or a possibility that the killer is talking directly to the press."

Mayor Daigle looked over at Detective Melancon, "Since this is your idea I want you be the one to run with it. I prefer that only one person talks to the press, that way we have better control over what gets released."

"Yes, sir. I have no problem talking to the editor at The Tribune." Jo wondered if she would get to speak with Bill Collins as well. For some unknown reason, being near him turned her insides to jelly.

***

Detective Picou wondered why this murderer believed this was a ritualistic killing. What made him think she was guilty of the deadly sin Pride?

Detective Picou's parents raised him Roman Catholic. He was familiar with the dynamics of the church and the teachings of the Bible. The killer's motives were beyond the realm of human comprehension. They had to figure out who was dishonoring the very belief of God before another innocent person was murdered!

If the killer was leaving them notes, then that meant he was not done. This was more than likely victim number one. Only their perpetrator knew how many he planned on killing. With Pride being one of the seven deadly sins, though, there was a chance they would be looking at seven victims, if not more. He needed to figure out what prideful act the killer believed the victim needed to repent for so that he could get into his (or her) mind. It could be almost anything; maybe she prided herself on the way she looked. What set this person off? What would drive a man, or woman, to commit such a vicious crime?

She was not murdered at her house or the crime scene. They still had to find the primary scene. Unfortunately, the rain washed away most of the evidence. Then there was the lack of evidence. The rain did not help, but Picou believed the killer cleaned the whole scene beforehand. If this were his first killing, it would mean that subsequent crime scenes would be just as hard to process. He already had his technique down and would only get better. The scary part was that when they started this good, it was almost impossible to catch them. Picou would not give up though. He would find this killer.

Could the perpetrator be trying to throw them off the trail? Maybe this was a love tryst gone wrong. This did not have the feeling of a murder committed by a jilted lover though.

Picou made plans for surveillance to be at the wake and funeral just in case the killer attended the services. The problem would be figuring out who it was. If the murderer were someone local, then they would more than likely attend the funeral anyway. Picou wanted to know who and who did not attend. He also wanted the names to go with the faces of everyone present. The husband had agreed to inform them if someone who did not belong showed up.

Picou decided to go home for the night. He needed a clear mind for in the morning if he wanted to catch this creep. Right now, they did not even have enough information to run through the FBI's Violent Criminal Apprehension Program, VICAP, for possible hits, except maybe the note. He planned to run the details of the note through VICAP in the morning.

***

As Melancon pulled up to her house, she noticed a shiny new black BMW in her driveway. She wondered who in the hell was waiting for her to arrive home. This had been a devil of a day, and all she wanted to do was fix herself a drink and relax. She heard a bottle of wine calling her name. She had stopped on the way home and bought a bowl of gumbo for supper. Even in this hot weather, she could eat Pierre's gumbo every night.

 As she parked in the driveway, she saw Bill Collins step out of the BMW. She let out a sigh of exasperation. What could he possibly want? She hadn't even talked to the editor at The Tribune so he couldn't know about the conversation they had with Mayor Daigle. If he did, then she knew there was a leak in the office.

"Detective Melancon, I'm sorry for stopping by but I was hoping to talk to you about the case."

Jo shook her head, "I have nothing to say to you about the case."

Bill was not satisfied with her reply, "I just have a few questions. Please, I promise not to take too much of your time."

"I guess I'm not going to get rid of you am I?"

He shook his head, "No, I'm not easy to get rid of."

She let out a sigh, "You may as well come in. I was going to talk to your editor in the morning about a proposition the Sheriff's Office has. I guess I'll talk to you while you are here?"

"Why Detective, I didn't take you for a woman that propositioned yourself."

She unlocked the door and shoved him inside, "Oh you. Come on inside. I was getting ready to eat supper. Pierre gave me extra gumbo if you want some."

He looked at her incredulously, "Gumbo? In this heat?"

"If you have ever had Pierre's gumbo, then you wouldn't ask that question." Melancon placed everything on the kitchen counter and asked, "Would you like something to drink? I think I have beer in the fridge. I am going to fix me a glass of merlot. I also have water and soda."

He picked up the bottle of merlot, "I can try a glass of wine I suppose. They say that a glass of red wine every night is good for the body."

She let out a soft laugh, "Then I may be on the right track."

Jo took out two wine glasses along with two bowls for the gumbo, "Would you mind opening the wine for us while I finish getting everything ready?"

As he opened the bottle, "I don't want you to go to any trouble. Honestly, I just came by to talk to you for a minute."

"Well, we can talk while we eat. I have not stopped all day, and I am starving. My mouth has been watering since I picked up the gumbo at Cherie's. Marie had fresh French bread and potato salad made too."

"Where exactly is Cherie's?"

"It's a bar not far from here, right off the highway."

Bill commented, "I didn't realize they sold food there."

"Well, technically they don't. The gumbo and sides are for the patrons. Pierre loves to cook as does Marie."

" I don't think I have ever stopped by there."

She looked him up and down, "No, I don't suppose you have."

"I'm not sure how to take that."

She smiled up at him, "It's just that most of the patrons at the bar are shrimpers and roughnecks. They aren't a bad crowd. They are down to earth, hard workers and old timers, who want a cold beer while they unwind and enjoy a game of cards."

"Sounds like my kind of place. I may just have to stop by."

Jo informed him, "On Friday nights there is a live band who plays really good Cajun music. Pierre has food almost every day."

She set the food in front of him at the kitchen bar, "Now what did you want to go over with me?"

"I wanted to talk to you about the investigation and your feelings on the killer. I've done my research and know that you have studied criminal behavior and psychology."

"And just how did you find all that out?"

Bill cleared his throat, "I have my sources. Let's just say the internet can be a very resourceful tool at times."

"Well, my education aside, I don't have that much information to give you right now. I was planning to talk to your editor tomorrow about a possible collaboration between The Tribune and the Sheriff's Office. We need to keep the public informed as much as possible, without the worry of creating mass panic."

"Well then that answers my question. My gut tells me that this may be a serial killer and if y'all want collaboration between the newspaper and the sheriff's office then y'all must feel the same way. I guess the mayor wants to prevent a public outcry after the Carl Ledet case."

Melancon responded, "You may not be far off in your thinking, but I can't go into too much detail about the case right now. I will tell you that this will be a win win situation for all involved."

By the time Bill left, Jo was dead tired on her feet. It was after one o'clock in the morning when she crawled in the bed. So much for her beauty sleep, she thought. She would be lucky if she got four hours of sleep and, right now, it was eluding her. For what felt like an eternity, all she could do was lay there and think about Bill Collins. Finally, fatigue won and she fell asleep.

When the alarm clock went off at six o'clock, she could barely open her eyes. She moved in slow motion as she showered and dressed. Walking into the kitchen, she prayed that she remembered to turn on the automatic coffee pot last night. The aroma of fresh coffee not only welcomed her, but also helped open her eyes.

Chapter 11
Greed

Eric headed to his study, unable to rest tonight. Smoke drifted from his Nording pipe as he settled in to read his paper. The aromatic scent of the pipe tobacco wafted through the room. He was unsettled tonight. He wandered over to the bar and poured himself a glass of Maker's Mark neat.

For a moment, he thought he heard something. Turning, he surveyed the room. He checked his elaborate security alarm to make sure no one was trying to break in. The room was empty. Only the ghosts of his past lurked in the murky recesses.

He took another puff on his pipe. He invited the smoke into his mouth for a moment before allowing the aroma to escape. That was better. He felt himself relaxing.

***

Night had long since fallen. Not a star was shining in the midnight sky. No moon hung to cast its warm glow. Darkness clutched the bayou in a grip as cold and black as death. Fog slithered among the cypress trunks like ghostly shadows. Hiding in the dark, one with the night, he patiently watched the house before him. This man he must set free was a serpent who spoke with a scheming tongue. He was a pupil of Lucifer himself.

He committed one of the seven deadly sins daily. Greed consumed him. Above all else, he had an inordinate desire to possess wealth and goods. He did not need everything he had. Everything this man owned was far beyond what dictated basic survival and comfort. He had an excessive amount of material wealth. He walked around town as though he was better than everyone else.

Eric Devareaux liked to dress with flair. He dressed to show off his wealth. He would never step into a department store to buy his suits; much less his socks and ties. Everything came from specialty businesses that catered to his every need. These stores had marble floors, brass doors and everything they sold was imported, up to date, and undeniably expensive. He refused to purchase it unless it stood out. Whatever he wore must make him stand out from everyone else.

Everything about Devareaux screamed money. He had no qualms about showing off his wealth. He believed that if you had it, you might as well flaunt it. When he died, he could not take it with him, and he was not going to leave it to a member of his family or a charity. Mais non, he would enjoy his time here on earth. He loved showing off his grandeur. His pride and joy though were his extravagant collection of cars. The multi-car garage attached to his house was full of various automobiles. The floor in there was pristine so that he could proudly walk around his collection savoring their raw power and beauty. He had a car for every day of the month. His collection ran from the vintage to the ultra-luxurious. He had a 1963 Ferrari 250 GTO, a 1966 Shelby Cobra 427, a 1965 Pontiac GTO, a 1991 Acura NSX, and a 1994 911 Porsche 3.6 Turbo Coupe to name a few.

He waited patiently for the Ketamine to kick in. He knew
Devareaux could not resist his nightly drink. He added more
than enough of the drug to the alcohol in case he only
poured himself a small nightcap.

Once the sinner passed out, he quickly made his move
before any police could arrive. He dragged Eric's limp body
to the pool and pushed him into the water. His graying hair
undulating as he floated in the water. Eric drank more of
the alcohol than he had thought. It would not take long for
him to drown.

Insects buzzed around him, and the water lapped gently
against the pool edge. He noticed neither. He stood at the
side of the pool staring at the dying man. It was so
appropriate that he drowned in his pool in his Armani suit
and Gucci leather oxfords.

He envisioned the people in town cheering over this man's
death. He had never met a greedier person. How many
people's lives had this man ruined here in Bear Corner while
he lived a life of luxury? How many people here had gone
hungry while he feasted on rich food and drank his blended
whiskey? No, no one here would mourn his death.

Something in the back of his head kept telling him that this
was wrong, this was murder. Mais non, this was God's will.
This man was a sinner. He committed one of the Seven
Deadly Sins, Greed.

It would be wrong to allow this man to walk this earth, to
steal from the poor while he lined his fat pockets.

Just looking through his house you could see how greedy he was, how omnipotent he thought he was. The house had polished marble everywhere and was adorned with Venetian Bronze fixtures. Mais non, he deserved this. He held material things close to his heart. Just looking around you could tell this home was a showplace. He had more money tied up in the bathroom than most people had in their whole house. While others struggled to make ends meet, he squandered their money on material things.

Fearing the cops may be here at any moment he recited as God instructed, "Dominus vobiscum."

Chapter 12

Picou was just sitting down at his desk when Melancon came up to him, "Got another body."

The muscles on the back of Picou's neck tightened, "Where?"

"Eric Devareaux's housekeeper found him floating in the pool this morning."

"Maybe it's not our killer."

Melancon shook her head, "Not the same type of MO, but the responding officer said he found a note near the pool."

"Damn, allons. I will drive. Is the coroner on his way?"

Melancon told him, "Dr. Harrison is on his way."

"Do we know if the scene has been disturbed?"

Melancon shook her head, "All I know is that when the responding officer found the note he secured the scene and called Sheriff Riley. I heard about it when I got in this morning. The housekeeper arrived not long ago. She said she waits until Mr. Devareaux leaves for work before she gets there. She was cleaning his study when she saw something in the pool. From what the officer said, she was pretty shaken up about finding his body."

Picou felt that jolt of adrenaline rush through his body when he had a killer to find. He assumed when he moved here that solving murders would be rare. In less than a year, he had had two serial killers on the loose. That was not good.

As they headed out to Picou's car Melancon asked, "You sure you don't want me to drive, mon ami?"

"Mais non, it's too early in the morning to have my heart stop." Picou had never met a woman who drove the way Melancon did. When he first transferred here, he let his partner drive to the crime scenes since she knew the way. After riding along with her for one week, he vowed to learn this small town like the back of his hand. She went from zero to sixty in no time flat. It did not matter if she was going a mile down the road, she sped to get there. She drove as if these roads were her own personal racetrack.

The morning fog was clearing as they arrived at the crime scene and parked in the circular drive of Mr. Devareaux's house, or mansion to be more precise.

Picou had never been to Devareaux's house and let out a whistle. Melancon grinned over at him, "This is nothing, you should see his car collection."

"I knew the man had money, but I didn't realize he had this kind of money."

Melancon stated, "It is old Louisiana money. His family has been in the banking business for several generations. Devareaux was a confirmed playboy and liked to spend the family money on himself and no one else."

Several cops were patrolling the area and setting up crime scene tape to cordon off the crime scene. A news van followed Picou and Melancon to the crime scene. Picou cussed the reporters under his breath even though he knew Mayor Daigle wanted them to work hand in hand with them. He looked over at Melancon, "Did you call the vultures?"

She watched as the news crew set up, "No, that's Channel 10. I have no idea how they found out about the murder so fast. Calling The Tribune is not a priority on my list right now. I figured it would be better if we did our job before having them plague us with questions we won't, or worse, can't answer yet."

Picou watched in disgust as the young anchor talked into the microphone almost as soon as she stepped out of the van.

He instructed the young officers standing out front, "The only words I want out of anyone's mouth are "No Comment" is that clear?"

They all answered, "Yes, sir," in unison. No one wanted to come under Detective Picou's wrath for talking to the press. Melancon and Picou bypassed the house and walked around back to the pool.

The stench of death, even in this early stage, was noticeable. Wanting to get started with this investigation, he headed over to the body, "Do you have a time of death doc?"

Dr. Harrison shook his head, "I won't have a definite answer until I do the autopsy, but I would say sometime after midnight. If it were not for the note, I would say he was drunk when he fell into the pool and accidentally drowned. I will run a blood alcohol level along with a Tox screen to see if he has any drugs in his system. There are no signs of a struggle."

The only thing linking these two victims was the note left behind. The note read, "Eric Devareux must repent for his GREED."

As Melancon read the note, she replied, "Mr. Devareaux's sin is no big surprise. Just about everyone in town, hell more than likely the state, knows the only thing on this man's mind is money. He did not care whom he had to stab in the back to make a dime. I've never met a greedier man."

It was highly unusual for the killer to change his MO. As Picou surveyed the scene, a crime scene tech working inside called out, "Detectives, we may have figured out why your killer didn't grab the man from his house."

Picou's curiosity was piqued. He followed Melancon inside. Officer Renault pointed to the computer screen, "Guy must have been paranoid. There are video cameras all over the house and property. If your killer had driven up to the house, it would have sounded all kinds of alarms. The alarm system is state of the art. If the phone line is cut, it automatically alerts the authorities and the owner."

Melancon let out a soft whistle, "Paranoid isn't the word for it. Our killer must have known about the security system ahead of time. I'm betting he stalks the victims, learns their patterns, and schedules before making his move."

Picou let out an exasperated sigh, "How in the hell are these two victims linked." It looked as if they may indeed be dealing with another serial killer. This was not what this town needed!

Chapter 13

He swallowed down a couple of ibuprofen for his pounding headache. However, this was turning into a full-blown migraine, and the ibuprofen would only dull the pain. It would have to do for now though.

He was still exhausted from this morning's activities. He somehow managed to push through his work and speak to people as though nothing out of the ordinary had happened. Nobody would guess he was guilty of murder. He had become proficient in making sure no one noticed anything out of the ordinary about him. He always had a cool demeanor about him.

He went about his business, eavesdropping when possible to the conversations going on around him. He even feigned surprise when asked about the recent murder. It seemed as if everybody was talking about the murders these days. Nobody talked about anything else. It upset him somewhat that no one talked about the sins these people committed. He wanted people to understand why they deserved to die.

So far, he had heard nothing he did not already know. He found the speculations amusing. Most of the theories that people came up with were absurd, still entertaining nonetheless.

Chapter 14

Mia stepped out of her bakery needing some fresh air. The weathered building that housed her bakery was located on the corner of Main and Jackson. The back of the bakery overlooked the bayou. The kitchen was off to one side of the building in order to give the dining room a view of the bayou. It had once been an elegant restaurant that, due to poor management, had failed. The location was perfect for a business. The old building still held its original embossed white tin ceilings reminiscent of the era in which it was built. While cleaning out a storage closet in the back of the kitchen, she found an antique cash register. After cleaning it, it now sat proudly on top of one of the glass display cases. Their actual cash register was hidden in a cabinet right behind it. Several glass display cases were arranged near the kitchen so that when they exited the kitchen with the treats they could put them directly into the case. The setup also allowed her to keep the flow of the main area nice and open. Guests could sit at the small bistro tables and enjoy the scenery.

The afternoon breeze was thick with humidity and melded with the aromas emitting from the various businesses along Main Street. The fragrance of her fresh coffee still lingered in the bakery, drifting outside. She could smell the gumbo the restaurant next door served daily, and it made her mouth water. She may just have to drop in and get her a bowl.

Thankfully, the breakfast crowd was long gone. The empty tables waited to be adorned with fresh tablecloths. She still needed to make the dough for tomorrow. If business kept increasing, she would have to hire more help. As it stood, she was already staying later and later preparing for the following day.

She was surprised to see how busy it was this afternoon. The UPS driver was steadily delivering packages. Several moms were out with their baby filled strollers enjoying the sunshine. Judge Holland was walking his little dog down the street.

She waved across the street to LouAnn Boutin at the flower shop, and reminded herself that she needed to go place this week's orders for flowers to use on the tables.

Mia was glad things were returning to normal after Carl Ledet's death. She still had nightmares and constantly checked to make sure no one was following her. She kept her doors locked. She was thankful for her parents, as well as Chad. And that Chad had been patient with her. He comforted her at night when she was too afraid to fall asleep. She could not help but feel secure when he wrapped his strong arms around her.

If it had not been for him and Jo then she would probably be the one buried in the graveyard instead of Carl Ledet.

As she walked over to talk to LouAnn, she caught the tail end of the conversation she was having with the UPS driver, "I'm telling you Eric Devareaux got what he deserved. Whoever said only the good died young never met that man. I have never met someone who was so money hungry. He'd steal from the blind."

Mia stood back, acting as if she was looking at the flowers. She had no desire to be part of this conversation. Too late, she heard LouAnn calling her, "Mia, Mia honey. Come tell this man about Eric Devareaux's body being found."

Mia let out a silent groan, not wanting to be part of this. "I'm sorry LouAnn I wasn't paying attention. I was looking at these beautiful flowers." Mia hoped that would change the subject.

"Mais oui, they are lovely aren't they? They just arrived this morning if you want me to fix you a bouquet."

"That would be lovely. I also need to go over what flowers to order for the tables this week. I think these may be quite charming."

"The hollyhocks are very nice, but let me show you the Asiatic Lilies. They are even lovelier. They are right over here, and they are the same price."

Mia let out a small sigh. It looked as if she had managed to change the subject. LouAnn asked, "So what do you think about Eric Devareaux being murdered."

Mia should have known it was too good to be true. "Who was killed? I'm sorry I don't seem to recognize that name."

LouAnn let out a gasp, "Mon Dieu, I assumed you would have been one of the first to have heard about the murder, what with Chad and you being married."

"Chad and I rarely talk about his work, especially after my ordeal with Carl Ledet."

"Oh Mo chagren! I am so sorry cher. It completely slipped my mind."

"I came by to place the order for the bakery. I just need simple arrangements for the tables."

"I think we can make a beautiful arrangement with some roses, baby's breath, Asiatic lilies and maybe a few other flowers."

Mia responded, "That sounds lovely. I want to keep it small, something simple." If Mia didn't watch it, she would have centerpieces bigger than the actual table. She found that flowers brightened the room and created a pleasant atmosphere.

"Of course, dear."

LouAnn went on to say, "I sure hope these recent murders don't keep your new husband away from you too much. Another murder is not the way to start out a workweek. Those poor men sure have had it rough lately. I swear it must be something in the water. We have never had trouble here in Bear Corner until recently, and now it seems as if we are cursed."

Mia would agree with that statement. It was as if the evil that surrounded Carl Ledet stayed around and infested another person here.

LouAnn continued on, "As much as I hate that someone was murdered, even someone like Eric Devareaux, I don't see many people shedding a tear over his death. He has been handing out foreclosure notices on quite a few hardworking families that have fallen on rough times. He refused to budge on any of the foreclosures."

Mildred Savoie piped in on the conversation, "Mais non, you won't find anyone that feels sorry for that man. He lived high on da hog dat one while the rest of us are fighting to scrape by. He would foreclose on ya without a second tought, mais yeah. Mais, I bet he would foreclose on his own parents, God rest their souls. It's a good ting dem two aren't alive to see what has become of dere son."

LouAnn stated, "He had ice in his veins that one. He would scare the devil himself."

Mildred continued, "Mais, dere may be a killer in town, but he has a definite agenda I tell you. None of dose two killed were stellar members of society."

A chill crawled up Mia's spine. She did not care what the person was like; having been on the receiving end of a psychotic killer, she did not wish that on anybody.

Mildred looked at Mia, "Mais, what did dat man of yours say. He's one of da police working on da case ain't he?"

"He hasn't talked about the killings. I only heard about this most recent one just now."

Mildred raised her arms up in the air, "Heaven help us if they ain't sharing anything with dey loved ones, what does dat mean? I tell you what dat means – they ain't going to tell us po' folks nothing."

LouAnn asked Mia, "Has he at least told you if they have suspects in the other murder?"

Mia shook her head, "I've been so busy with the bakery that I haven't had time for anything else. We try not to discuss police business. The sheriff doesn't like information getting out in these cases."

Mildred let her opinion known, "Mais it was Victoria Russo's husband dat killed her I tell you. He is a two timing son of a gun. Couldn't keep it in his pants, mais non."

As much as the people hated Eric Devareaux, her heart went out to him. She suspected that he did not die an easy death. The list of people that wanted him dead was staggering. Chad and Jo had their work cut out for them. She had a feeling until this murderer was caught, she would not be seeing much of her husband. She hoped they could at least see each other, even if it was just in passing, during the day. They did not even know if the same person that killed Victoria killed Eric Devareaux.

As Mia headed home, she was glad her life had finally righted itself. She was so thankful that Chad did not mind moving in here. As soon as she stepped into this house, she had fallen in love with it. Initially, it was a little larger than she needed, but now that she was married, she could picture raising a family here with Chad. The house not only had her dream kitchen, but it was large, spacious and had almost every amenity anyone could want. The kitchen, dining room, and living room were one great room that overlooked the bayou. There were two smaller bedrooms along with a large master bedroom. Mia turned one of the bedrooms into a guest room and the other into her office. The previous owner even built a magnificent outdoor kitchen into the screened in back porch. She could either cook indoors or out. It was as if this house had been made for her, and now she shared it with Chad.

Chapter 15

Sheriff Riley sat at his desk in his office and stared out the window that overlooked the marshland behind the office. From here, he could see the boathouse and the boats that belonged to the Sheriff's Office.

Being a sheriff for a close-knit community was usually fairly straightforward. He made sure to know the residents and what went on around town.

This case, though, had him stumped. He thought he knew what skeletons everyone had hidden in their closets, and he was finding out that just was not true. He had a hard time picturing anyone he grew up with capable of committing these heinous crimes.

Sheriff Riley groaned when he heard the intercom go off. He hated the blasted thing most of the time. This time, however, he was glad to have a warning. The buzz of the intercom could only mean one thing, "Sorry to bother you, sir, but the mayor is here to see you." Mais oui, he knew it. His day deteriorated in a matter of minutes. He did not need this man telling him how he should be doing his job.

"Send him back." Getting up from his desk, he opened the door to greet Mayor Daigle.

After shaking hands, Sheriff Riley gestured for the mayor to take a seat, as he shut the door and sat behind his desk. Clearing his throat, Mayor Daigle somberly said, "Morning, Sheriff. I'm guessing you know why I am paying you this visit today. Sure wish it were under different circumstance."

Sheriff Riley could not help but agree, "Same here, sir. These killings are at the worst possible time. Everything was settling down after the Carl Ledet matter and now this. We can't seem to catch a break lately. We are not even sure if Eric Devareaux was killed by the same person as Victoria Russo. A lot of people around here despised that man."

Mayor Daigle asked, "And you are sure that Mrs. Russo's husband had nothing to do with her death?"

"Mais non, he has an airtight alibi. He was with his mistress. The hotel manager and a maître d at the restaurant confirmed that he was in Springport at the time of his wife's death. He could have hired someone to kill her, but this was not a hired hit. Besides, what did he have to gain by her death? She had a life insurance policy, but it wasn't a substantial amount for him."

Mayor Daigle nodded his head in agreement, " I understand you have Detectives Melancon and Picou working on the case."

"Yes, sir, they are. I am more than conformable with them handling this case."

Mayor Daigle replied, "Mais non, that's not what I meant. I was just going to ask if we needed to approve overtime or hire extra officers to help patrol the town."

"That sure would be nice. Do we have the funds for that?"

"I don't think I will have any problems getting the town council to agree right now. I would rather keep crime down and after the Carl Ledet case it should be easy to push hiring extra personnel through."

"Then I say let's do it."

"Now, what about this case? Do we have any new updates?"

Sheriff Riley leaned back in his chair and folded his arms across his chest, "Detective Melancon is at the courthouse right now finding out who had foreclosure liens filed. We are still waiting for forensics to complete their reports, but so far, the list of suspects in these murders is staggering. They both had an enemy or two, possibly more. A complete sweep was done of the crime scene. They dusted for fingerprints and gathered trace evidence. Now it is being sorted through. So far all of the prints have been accounted for. Each person had a reason to be there which could mean that the killer was someone they knew. This would fit with why there was no forced entry."

"What about cause of death?"

Sheriff Riley responded, "Dr. Harrison is running a tox screen on him right now. There is a chance that he was drugged beforehand. There was water in his lungs, so we know he was alive when he hit the water. The other victim had a sedative in her system called Ketamine. On the street, it is called Special 'K'. It is easily obtainable. If Eric Devareaux has it in his system, then it is safe to say we are dealing with the same killer."

Running it through his mind, Mayor Daigle said, "The only problem is that Eric Devareaux was a hated man. A lot of people wanted him dead. Do you believe we have a serial killer running loose?”

“I sure as hell hope not. If we do have a killer with a set mission, he is probably smart enough to wait until things die down before striking again.”

Chapter 16

Jo was anxious about talking to Bill Collins again. When he looked at her with that sexy smile on his face, she felt her knees grow weak. He was getting to her, and she had no choice but to work with him on this case.

She did not understand why he intrigued her, but something about him pushed her to delve deeper into his life. She sensed something lurking behind that easygoing veneer he showed the world. She was playing with fire. The man was trouble. Besides, she did not need to start a relationship with someone she would be working with. That made way for even more trouble.

Just the thought of Bill next to her sent her heart racing. Her dreams were becoming a little raw when they involved him, which made it more difficult to be calm and professional when she had to work with him.

Besides, she was getting way ahead of herself. He probably wasn't even interested in her and if he was, then what? Right now, all she had time for was casual sex. With an active investigation going on, she didn't have time for commitment, romance, and candlelight dinners.

 She was not sleeping at night. This case stayed on her mind. Every time she closed her eyes, she saw the victims. Jo took a deep breath. She needed to take her mind off of these cases. If she weren't meeting Bill at her house, she would go to Cherie's to knock back a few and forget. Maybe she could even find someone there who wanted to have wild, passionate sex with no attachments.

She did not see Bill being that person. Not that there was anything wrong with him. She had a feeling he would be very satisfying in bed.

She'd barely made it home when she heard the doorbell ring. Bill was at the door, "I figured you didn't have time to eat so I picked us up a pizza for supper while we talk about the case."

She caught a whiff of the delicious aroma, "That smells fantastic. Come on in. Do you want a beer?"

Bill placed the pizza on the counter, "That sounds great. I heard you had a lousy day."

Jo opened up the two beers, handing him one, "That is putting it mildly. The list of suspects who wanted to see Eric Devareaux dead is astounding. I never knew how many enemies he had."

Jo watched as Bill grabbed himself a slice of pizza, "So do you think these two murders are related?"

Suddenly an image of Bill holding her in his arms and devouring her with kisses flashed through her mind. She took a swallow of beer and forced her mind to clear. "I can't give you all the details, but yes, we believe they are."

Bill contemplated what she was telling him, "What is the connection between the two victims?"

Jo bit into a slice of pizza and savored the flavor. "So far, we have not been able to link them. They traveled in some of the same social circles, but that is about it. We have not found any evidence that they crossed paths. Right now the only thing that is linking these two together is the killer."

She could see the wheels turning in Bill's head, "Here's the thing. How did the killer know about Russo fooling around on his wife?"

"That's just it. Mr. Russo has said that he kept it quiet and that Victoria was okay with the affair as long as he let her spend money and did not complain. From the looks of their financial records, she went through money as if it was water. Russo has an airtight alibi."

Bill asked, "Did Russo say who knew he was out of town?"

Jo helped herself to another slice of pizza, "He said that it wasn't a big secret that he would be out of town. Victoria had talked about his upcoming trip to practically everyone."

"Why did the killer stage the first body and not Devareaux's?"

Jo contemplated how much she should divulge to Bill, "I have a feeling it was harder for our killer to get close to Devareaux. This has to stay off the record for now, but his alcohol may have been poisoned."

"So then this was premeditated?"

Jo looked up at him, "Yes, but this killer had to know some intimate details about him. He had security measures in place that rival Fort Knox."

As Bill ate another slice of pizza, he thought about what she'd just told him. That would fit with Devareaux's paranoia, "But who would know about the security system. I have been to his house several times for parties and trust me he never announced the security system. The only thing he boasted about was how much money he spent on the luxuries in his life."

Jo nodded her head in agreement, "Everyone I have talked to so far has confirmed that his life was led by greed."

"Money was everything to him. He would probably sell his first born to make a buck. Status was everything to him."

"The question of the day is who hated the man enough to actually kill him?"

"Mon ami, that is why you are the detective. Which leads me to my next question, what made you want to become a police officer?"

Jo thought about the question for a moment, "It's in my blood I guess. My grandfather was on the force, and I always loved hearing his stories. My dad is a shrimper and as much as I love him, fishing never interested me. Growing up, I played cops and robbers with my brothers and cousins so the job came naturally to me."

Bill let out a laugh, "I can see you running around the yard with a toy gun."

Jo grinned over at him, "We weren't that fortunate to have toy guns. We found sticks in the yard that we thought resembled guns and used our imagination."

"Even better. So I'm guessing you were a tomboy."

Jo laughed at the memories, "My mom wanted a little girl. She dressed me up in pink frilly dresses, and I ran around in the yard as if it were a T-shirt and pair of shorts. She never gave up on the hope that I would attend dance classes and be the little girl she had dreamed of having."

"And now?"

Jo shrugged her shoulders, "Now, she has gotten used to the idea that I am a cop. She is not happy about it and is always trying to get me to change careers, but I believe she has come to accept that it won't happen. I wish my grandfather were alive so he could see what I have become."

"I'm sure he is looking down at you beaming with pride."

Jo polished off her last bite of pizza and asked, "Did you always want to be a reporter?"

Bill shook his head, "Actually no. At first, I wanted to be an attorney, but while I was in a prelaw class, I had an assignment on researching a case. I enjoyed researching and writing about the details, so the next day I talked to the counselor about changing my curriculum."

"I've read some of your work, which is why you were chosen to collaborate with the Sheriff's Office. You have a way with words."

Bill finished his beer, "I've always been a great bull shitter. That is one of the most important things in this business."

"You don't seem to be as pushy as some of the other journalists."

He shrugged his shoulders, "I'm just seasoned I guess. I worked in New Orleans and Baton Rouge for a while before settling down here."

"What made you come back home?"

Bill responded, "My mom was diagnosed with cancer, and I wanted to be close by in case she or dad needed me.

"But I also needed my own space, so I bought a house. We would have gotten on each other's nerves if I lived with them. When Mom had a bad day or night, I would stay with her. After she passed away, I couldn't leave my dad, so I stayed here instead of moving back to New Orleans."

Jo enjoyed listening to what Bill had to say and found it intriguing that he had a human side.

"So you are the one that bought the old Carmichael plantation?"

"I got it for a hell of a price and couldn't pass it up. I have grand plans for fixing it up, but I just haven't found the time."

Jo asked, "I take it you are a handy man as well?"

Bill let out a laugh, "I'm learning. That is probably why it is taking me so long to make any headway on the project. Most Saturdays I keep the television on one of the home improvement channels hoping to learn how to do something. I may have to hire a contractor if I want to get any work done."

"I'm impressed that you even considered taking on such a monumental task. If I remember correctly, that house is huge."

"It is a monstrosity. But if you look past the work that needs to be done on it, you can still see the grandeur of the place. I was lucky that the previous residents left a good bit of furniture. I've been slowly restoring that as well."

"You may have a new career on your horizon."

Bill shook his head, "Not likely. However, it has been a learning experience. It also gives my dad something to do to keep his mind off my mother's death. Some days he spends hours over there piddling around on one project or another while I am at work."

Jo loved hearing his deep voice, it sent shivers down her spine. He looked down at his watch and sighed, "I guess I need to let you get to bed, and I need to finish writing my article."

As she walked him to the door, she found herself wishing he could stay longer. Opening the door, she told him, "It was nice talking to you tonight. Thanks for the pizza."

"You are welcome, any time you need supper give me a call, and we can talk about the case in more detail."

Jo felt her heart sink at that comment. As she watched him drive off, she wondered if the case was the only reason he was talking to her.

Chapter 17

Melancon sat down at her desk with a cup of coffee and The Tribune. She was anxious to see what Collins wrote.

Killer Took Second Victim

The Bear Corner Sheriff's Office confirmed that an unknown killer has claimed a second victim's life. Eric Devareaux was found floating in his pool by his housekeeper.

The Sheriff's Office is waiting for the toxicology reports to come back, but they suspect that the same person murdered Victoria Russo and Eric Devareaux. Victoria Russo had a sedative called ketamine, known as "Special K" on the streets, in her system.

Unfortunately for the Bear Corner Sheriff's Office, the list of suspects who wanted to see Eric Devareaux dead is staggering. Mr. Devareaux was the president of the bank and had no qualms about foreclosing on the residents here in Bear Corner.

Melancon looked up from the newspaper when she heard someone at her desk, "Officer DuPuy, is there something I can help you with."

"I have the preliminary report on the names you gave me to cross-reference. The list isn't as long as we thought it would be."

Melancon was impressed, "How late did you stay last night working on this?"

"I left around midnight. I figured I would get back to work on it after a good night's sleep. But when I made it home, I could not sleep so I worked on it some more. I may have to put out an APB on the truck that ran over me last night though."

Melancon smiled at the young officer, "If you find that truck let me know. The same one hit me. I can't get this case out of my mind either."

Melancon perused the list, "Did any names stand out to you when you were going over it?"

Officer DuPuy shook his head, "Nothing at all. I could not find anything that linked the two victims. I wonder if the connection is in the killer's mind. If it weren't for the notes, would you even suspect they were killed by the same person?"

Melancon looked over the information he had handed her one more time, "No, the note is the only thing that links the murders. We are still waiting to see if Devareaux had Ketamine in his system. Victoria Russo was tortured before she was killed. Eric Devareaux got lucky, and he drowned in his pool. Neither victim had defensive wounds on their bodies. I'm wondering if they knew their killer personally since the notes left behind contained private details no one else seemed to know. The notes alone lead me to believe that our killer is just getting started."

Chapter 18

Mia tried her best to wait up for Chad to get home, but she fell asleep. She awoke to a warm wet heat developing inside of her.

She felt warmth surround her nipple as a tongue played with the taut bud. Warm fingers teased the other nipple. Tugging gently and squeezing. She moaned in delight and looked into Chad's eyes.

His mouth grew more urgent against hers. She felt the warmth of his body stretched against hers. His hands caressed and kneaded, sending tingles of delight down her body. She arched her body to his as he teased her. The hair on his legs tickled her silky legs. She felt his erection pressing into her.

He nuzzled her neck, sending waves of desire through her body. He cupped her breasts, massaging and stroking her nipples. His hands moved lower down her body, stroking and caressing her inner thighs. Goosebumps covered her body. He played with her, teasing and taunting her. Desire cut her to the core. An inferno burned through her. She writhed in delight as he slowly caressed her. He teased her relentlessly. His touch was rapturous torture. The pleasure was overwhelming.

She was riding a wave of ecstasy between her legs. His tongue and lips gently teased her as new waves of pleasure coursed through her. His tongue delved into her, swirling around. She climbed higher and higher as pleasure built inside of her.

He whispered in her ear, "You are so beautiful. I love pleasing you." She kissed him with intense passion. Chad ravished her with his mouth.

She could take no more, "Chad I need you now."

In one swift movement, he was inside her. He rode her harder than he ever had before. He thrust deeper and deeper inside of her. Her body convulsed around him as they both found their release at the same time.

Afterwards, she curled into him, "I'm glad you made it home."

He pulled her tighter to him, and they drifted off to sleep.

Chapter 19

Detective Jo Melancon walked out of the courthouse and looked up at the sky. The list of the impending foreclosures that Eric Devareaux filed was staggering for this small community. Their list of possible suspects was endless. Just about everyone wanted him dead.

She stopped by the vendor that worked at the corner of the courthouse to purchase a hot dog before heading back to the Sheriff's Office. She may as well eat now because she had a feeling that when she got back it would be nonstop.

As soon as she got back to the office, she reviewed her messages and returned phone calls while checking her emails. Afterwards, she studied the file one more time. She did not understand how there could be no fingerprints, no evidence, and no results back yet on the tox screen. She could see the pool water washing away some trace evidence, but there had to be something around the pool. Surely this unsub could not be this lucky.

Melancon had already talked to Devareaux's secretary, and she confirmed that plenty of people had been upset with him. However, she didn't recall anyone making a direct threat against him. They had gone through his emails, phone messages, and text messages and found plenty of hate mail, but no one directly came out and threatened to kill him.

Picou walked over to her desk, "You look as frustrated as I feel."

"Whoever killed these two knew what they were doing. They covered their tracks well. There was no solid evidence found at either scene. The list of suspects in Devareaux's case is overwhelming. That man had more enemies than you could shake a stick at, but so far, none of them hated him enough to kill him. Hell, everyone I have talked to was shocked that someone killed him, but not surprised someone had wanted to."

Picou informed her, "Watch out when you step outside. The press is camped outside the station."

"Great, I don't want to deal with them right now. They will want answers that we don't have."

Chapter 20

Sheriff Riley, Detectives Picou and Melancon along with several of the other police officers were all meeting in the conference room. Sheriff Riley shut the door after the last person entered. The Sheriff looked over at Detective Picou, "So let me get this straight, no forensic evidence was gathered at the scene. Are we any closer to bringing in a possible suspect to talk to?"

Picou stated, "No, sir. We do know that Victoria Russo had no defensive wounds on her body, which means she did not put up a fight. There were sedatives found in her tox screen. It appears that Devareaux was drugged before either falling or being forced into the pool. Once again, there were no defensive wounds. We know neither of these victims put up a fight."

Chapter 21
Wrath

If there was anyone that could be considered perfect for the deadly sin of wrath, it was Attorney Graham Easterly. He had never seen someone more deserving of dying before. Attorney Easterly's wife, Sandra, could swear all she wanted that she was a klutz, but he knew what those bruises meant. Her husband took his anger out on her.

He stood by the attorney's black BMW and craned his neck to see if anyone was watching. Remaining inconspicuous, he bent down and unscrewed the plastic cap on the tire valve system. He punctured a small enough hole for the air to leak out. It took under a minute to complete the task.

Standing, he surveyed the parking lot once again. No one seemed to notice him.

He had been observing Graham Easterly's movements over the last two weeks, and this was his best chance of getting him alone. If he timed this right, the tire would go flat on a stretch of deserted bayou land as Mr. Easterly headed to his mistress's house. He had no doubt that the cheating husband would call his wife to tell her he was working late. No one would pay attention to a Good Samaritan stopping to help someone with a flat tire. The stun gun in his pocket was ready to go.

***

Graham picked up his phone and called his wife to tell her now he was working late and not to wait up for him. On his way to Sheila's house, he stopped by the local florist to pick up the dozen yellow roses he had ordered. The fragrant flowers filled his car with their heady scent. He thought about how Sheila would thank him for the gift.

Graham saw the warning light on his dashboard informing him of a low tire. He groaned at the prospect of having to get out and change a tire. Now he regretted being too cheap to invest in the run flat tires, and he couldn't call someone out to change his tire. He could have no proof that he was anywhere but at his office. He would have to change the tire so he could get over to Sheila's house. Just the thought of her waiting on him gave him an erection. She was nowhere near as lovely as his wife was, but Sheila had no qualms about playing the games he liked to play. His wife, however, turned up her pert little nose at his desires.

Getting out of the car, he noticed that the road was deserted. He was grateful for that minor miracle. He did not need someone seeing him over this way and telling his wife. She would want to know why he was here instead of at the office or home. If she caught him cheating on her again, she would take him for everything he had.

The warm air hit him as soon as he stepped out of his car. The stars were brilliant tonight, but he was in no mood to enjoy the night sky. As he headed to the trunk of the car, he muttered to himself, bad temperedly. He could not believe all the luck of getting a damn flat tire, and he was in his best suit.

As he popped open the trunk of the car his gray eyes surveyed his surroundings one more time. A breeze blew through his black hair that was starting to show a few strands of gray. He considered coloring his hair to remove any evidence of gray, but Sheila liked it so he decided to leave it. She thought it made him look even more distinguished. Even at his age, he was still a good looking man. He was over six feet tall, had a chiseled chin and jawline, strong shoulders, and a trim waist.

Sandra reminded him constantly that he was a handsome man. She tried to keep him on a short leash, but he managed to find time for a mistress on the side.

Graham jumped at the sound of a man walking up behind him. He never even saw the lights of a vehicle, much less heard anything. The man walked over to him, "Do you need a hand sir?"

He snapped his head towards the stranger, apparently not wanting the intrusion, "Damn, do you think you could have at least honked when you pulled up behind me? Why didn't you keep your lights on? You scared the hell out of me. Damn tires! I should be good, won't take me long."

"It would go faster with some help."

Graham looked around trying to place where he was. His mind was a blur right now. He struggled to remember what happened. He was in the dark. He had a hard time telling if it was daylight outside. How long was he out? He was completely unaware of time.

He tried to sit up, and panic took over his body when he realized his arms and legs were restrained. He pulled on them with all his might, but the restraints refused to budge.

He heard footsteps moving closer to him. "Who is there? Show yourself?"

Overhead lights came on, blinding him. He saw his captor. There was something vaguely familiar about him, "What do you want? Why am I tied down?"

He leered down at him, "You are a sinner and must atone for your sins. Are you ready to repent?"

"What in the hell are you talking about? What sins must I atone for?"

He picked up the knife, "You and I both know what sins you have committed? You have committed one of the seven deadly sins, wrath, and now you must pay for your sins?"

"Listen you son of a bitch, I don't know who you think you are but I answer to no one."

His captor brought the knife closer to him, "Oh, but that is where you are wrong. You must answer to God for your sins. Are you ready to answer to God?"

In one swift movement, pain ravaged Graham as the man cut off his private parts. Blood gushed against his thighs. The pain was so intense that it astounded him.

The man who did this loomed above him, holding his manhood in his hands.

All signs of arrogance disappeared from the vengeful man's eyes, which seemed to beg for mercy. "You have to pay for your sins."

He gasped out, "You bastard."

In calmness, his captor told him, "You must be punished for your sins."

His pulse was pounding. He swallowed hard. He was not sure if it was from the pain rushing through his body or fear, but cold beads of sweat formed along his forehead. "I haven't done anything so wrong that I deserve this."

"Oh, but you have mon ami."

Easterly glared at this lunatic, "I am not your friend."

"Mais non, you are a sinner. You must confess your sins in order to repent. God knows what sins you have committed, and He has told me that it is my mission to make you repent for those sins."

The pain and loss of blood made it difficult to stay conscious. He tried to grasp what this lunatic was talking about. He kept mumbling on and on about sin, redemption and punishment.

As the life left Easterly's body, he recited, "Dominus vobiscum." He ran his thumb over his forehead, chin, and chest in the sign of the cross to give him absolution.

***

How poignant that he captured this sinner on his way to see his mistress. The whole town would know about her when his body was found on her front lawn. He wondered if his wife knew about the house he'd purchased for his mistress.

Chapter 22

Melancon heard her phone ringing. She groaned when she saw that it was the dispatcher calling, "Melancon."

"Sorry to wake you Detective but we have another body."

Melancon looked over at her alarm clock and noticed that it was almost four o'clock in the morning, "Where is the body?"

"178 Morningview Lane. You will never guess who it is?"

A chill swept through Melancon's body, "Who?"

"Attorney Graham Easterly."

That statement helped wake Melancon up, "Graham Easterly lives clear on the other side of town."

"I have a feeling the mistress called it in. When I took the call, I looked up the address to see who owns the property. Sheila Graves owns it, but the tax assessor has that it was paid for by Graham Easterly."

Melancon knew the man was a snake in the grass, but it looked as if he was keeping him a playmate right under his wife's nose. "Send an officer to the Easterly's house to make sure that his wife is there. Tell him to snoop around, but I want to be the one to tell her about her husband. That way we can see if she is genuinely upset."

"I will send Officer Zerinque to watch their house and let you know if she comes or goes."

"Thanks. Have you called Detective Picou yet to let him know about the body?"

"Not yet. I saw that you were on call last night."

Melancon informed him, "That's fine. I'll call him."

Melancon knew that Easterly's murder was huge. Especially if it turned out his body was on his mistress's door front. Apparently someone knew about the affair, but who? She wondered if the same person was responsible for this.

She called Picou, "Rise and shine big boy. Another sinner has been murdered."

Picou groaned, "Who was it this time?"

"Your favorite attorney, Graham Easterly. It looks as if his body was left on his mistress's door step."

"Damn, I knew the man was a snake in the grass, but I didn't know he had a mistress. Isn't his wife some fox or something."

Melancon informed him, "Oh yeah, all the men in town drool over her. But his body was left at Sheila Graves's doorstep."

Now that surprised Picou, "So he was banging Sheila Graves here in town."

"Oh yeah, and he may have purchased the house for her."

Picou exclaimed, "Damn, this is getting better and better. Who would have known that the man was cheating on his wife and with whom?"

"I don't know, but there will be some interesting interviews today."

"Let's see what the mistress has to say first since the body was found there. Then we can go talk to the wife afterwards."

***

Mia sleepily propped herself on her pillow, "I take it there was another body?"

Picou leaned over and kissed her before jumping in the shower, "Yep. Graham Easterly was found dead this morning. At least now I have a connection between the murder victims. Devareaux and Easterly were cohorts. Easterly handled most of Devareaux's legal business. I need to see where Victoria Russo fits into this though. As far as I know they ran in the same social crowd, but that is about it. Russo was a stay at home wife who spent her time shopping. I don't think she ever worked."

"This is kind of scary, though. Do you think Victoria could have been killed to throw you off?"

"I don't know, but there has to be a connection somewhere. I need to get a shower and head out."

"What if it is about sinners? What if this guy wants to take up where Ledet left off?"

"I think Ledet had his own agenda. But there is a strong possibility that we may have another killer with a religious angle though. Something tells me that he is not done. This killer knows very personal details about these victims' lives.

I need to figure out who that is." Picou did not tell Mia that Easterly's body was found at his mistress's house. Who knew about the affair? This was a small town and Picou had never heard any rumors regarding Graves and Easterly seeing each other. They were damn careful.

He needed to find out if Easterly or Graves might have mentioned their affair to someone in passing. Now if the wife knew about the affair that complicated matters and broadened the suspect list.

They needed to find out if the realtor knew that Easterly bought the house for his mistress and if he paid cash for it or if there was a mortgage.

***

They had another victim with a long list of enemies. She assumed his sin would have something to do with his practice. Easterly and Devareaux were friends, and he filed most of the foreclosures for Devareaux. Someone had done their homework.

She thought that Graham and Sandra were a happily married couple. It appeared that you never knew what went on behind closed doors. If his wife did not know he was cheating on her and had even purchased a house for his mistress, he was probably better off dead. When they talked to the wife later on all hell might break loose.

By the time she arrived at Sheila Graves' house, the crime scene techs were already there working the scene. Dr. Harrison was also there.

Picou asked, "Does it look like it's our killer?"

Dr. Harrison nodded his head, "Found your note stuck to the body, "Graham Easterly must repent for WRATH." He did a number on his body. So far, the only one who got off lucky was Devareaux. I have to warn you that this kill was worse than the first."

Picou stared down at the body, and he felt the cold sweat break out along his forehead, "Lord, have mercy this killer isn't playing around is he?"

Melancon felt her knees weaken when she saw the body. "Oh my God!" Melancon thought she was prepared, but when she saw the body, she felt the earth move. "Is that what I think it is?"

Dr. Harrison said grimly, "Yep, your killer cut off the entire male organ and placed it in his mouth."

The grisly sight was more than Melancon could take. The image was one she would never forget. "Please tell me there were at least some hesitation marks?"

Dr. Harrison shook his head, "No, I am beginning to think your guy has some medical knowledge. The cut is smooth. He removed Easterly's penis and testicles in one very precise move. I also believe the attorney was alive when it happened. There is a good bit of blood between his thighs, which indicates blood was still pumping through the body when it was removed."

Picou shuddered at the thought. Their killer could have just removed the penis, but instead he chose to remove the whole package to stick in the guy's mouth. "What about the other wounds?"

"It looks as if the rest were done in a frenzy to be honest with you. This was another dumpsite. I will run a tox panel to see if he has any special 'K' in his system. Mr. Easterly was a big man, though, and I do not see him going along with this. He would have put up a fight."

Officer Rouchon approached quickly, "I'm sorry to bother y'all, but we found Mr. Easterly's car. Someone tried pushing it off the side of the road, but not enough to hide it completely. It looks as if he had a flat tire while he was on his way here."

Melancon looked over at Picou, "It looks like we may know how he got to Attorney Easterly then." She turned to Officer Rouchon, "Have the car towed to the garage so that the forensic techs can go over it with a fine tooth comb. I want to see if that flat was deliberate."

"Yes, ma'am." Officer Rouchon excused himself to let them finish their business with Dr. Harrison while he got busy with the car. He could not help but cringe when he looked at the dead body. At first he was not sure, but a second look confirmed that the man had his family jewels crammed into his mouth. He shuddered when he thought about the pain that involved.

As the techs were preparing to remove the body, Picou told them, "Make sure you bag the hands. Graham Easterly would have tried to fight off his attacker. Maybe we will get lucky and find some evidence under his nails. With this amount of mutilation, maybe we will catch a break in the case. Hopefully, our perp cut himself in the process."

Dr. Harrison nodded his head at the techs to continue what they were doing. "Detective Picou, the body is in good hands. I won't let anything drop. Everything you want is standard for cases such as this."

Picou shook his head, "I don't mean to belittle you. I know you are damn good at your job, but I want to stop this bastard before he kills again. One missed detail could let this killer get away. "

Sheriff Riley came to stand by Detectives Melancon and Picou as the ME's office removed the body from the crime scene, "Looks like we got us a serial killer on our hands."

Picou shook his head, "I think we have a murderer who has a very definite plan on our hands. He is on a mission, and only he knows what it is. He has left notes on each body stating that they were sinners and which sin they committed.

Sheriff Riley contemplated what Picou said, "These three may have run in the same social circles, but I don't think Victoria Russo was friends with either man."

Melancon stated, "Someone wanted these people to pay for their sins, and they wanted us to know that they have sinned. This cold, calculating killer drugs the victim so that he can incapacitate them before killing them. Whoever is doing this most likely knew that Mr. Russo was having an affair, and Victoria didn't care. Everyone in town knew that Devareaux only cared about money, but then almost no one knew about the affair between Easterly and Graves. This is someone privy to these secrets, and we need to figure out who it is."

Picou knew Melancon was right in her thinking, but who would have knowledge of this information? Neither man was going around talking about his affair.

Picou asked Melancon, "Are you ready to go talk to Sheila Graves?"

"As ready as I will ever be."

As they walked into the house, they saw Sheila sitting on the couch with tissues crumpled up around her. Mascara streaked down her face, and her eyes were red and swollen. As soon as she saw them, she barraged them with questions, "Just how many people have to die before you stop this monster?"

Melancon tried to put her at ease, "Ms. Graves we are very sorry for your loss." Even after the words left her mouth, she knew they sounded hollow, but nothing they said would make her feel better. "Did you hear anything at all last night or early this morning?"

The woman's lower lip quivered, "When Graham didn't show up last night I tried calling him, but my calls went straight to voicemail. I assumed his wife gave him grief about not being home, so he had to go appease her instead of coming here. Sandra kept a tight leash on him, so it was hard for Graham to get away. I stayed up late last night just in case he decided to come over, but must have fallen asleep. Around three o'clock a noise woke me. I thought maybe Graham was here, and when I opened my door, I found him." Sheila let out a heartbreaking sob, "Who could have done something so cruel?"

Melancon took her hand in hers, "Ms. Graves I need to ask you something very personal, who knew you were having an affair with Graham?"

"No one that I can think of. Graham pulled into the garage with his lights off. He made sure he did not come over until it was dark outside to keep from being noticed. He stressed to me that we had to keep this quiet, that if his wife found out he would be a dead man." Sheila let out a gasp, "Oh no, you don't think the killer is Sandra do you?"

Picou shook his head, "No, whoever did this had some serious upper body strength. Mr. Easterly's body was dead weight, and I don't see Mrs. Easterly manhandling his body."

"I realize people believe Graham and Eric Devareaux got what they deserved, but Graham was a good man. He didn't deserve this."

Melancon kept her mouth shut. A good man did not cheat on his wife. She placed her hand on Sheila's shoulder, "We will do everything we can to find out who killed these people. This person will be brought to justice."

Picou asked Sheila, "Have you noticed any unfamiliar vehicles in the neighborhood lately. Maybe any unusual activity around your place?"

Sheila shook her head, "I haven't, but I'm sure that there are a few nosy neighbors around here. Maybe someone saw something."

Picou decided to have some of the patrol officers go house to house to see if any of the neighbors noticed anything out of the ordinary. This guy found out that these two were having an affair somehow, and he knew exactly where to leave the body.

Chapter 23

Melancon and Picou went to Sandra Easterly's house together. Picou told Melancon, "I'll let you break the news to the wife."

"Gee thanks, buddy."

Picou gave her a grim smile, "Maybe it will come across better coming from another woman."

"I don't think there is an easy way to deliver this information. I wonder if she knew about the affair."

Sandra Easterly heard the doorbell ring and wondered who was here. Graham did not come home last night, and she had been trying to get in touch with him. He said he would be working late, but she never imagined that he would sleep at the office. She saw the two officers standing by the front door and knew whatever news they were here to tell her could not be good. Her stomach clenched in dread as she opened the door. Had Graham been in a bad accident, or worse, were they here to offer their condolences? She braced herself for what they were about to tell her.

"Officers, can I help you with something?"

Melancon spoke up, "Mrs. Easterly we are with the Bear Corner Sheriff's Office. I am Detective Jo Melancon and this is Detective Chad Picou. May we come in?"

Sandra opened the door to let them pass. She quickly pulled down the sleeves of her shirt, but not before Jo caught a glimpse of the bruise she was trying to hide. "Mrs. Easterly is your husband home?"

"No, Graham called last night to say he would be working late. I guess he spent the night at the office. I've been trying to reach him, but he isn't answering his phone."

Melancon placed her hand on the poor woman's shoulder, "Mrs. Easterly, why don't we go sit down." Sandra paled as she looked at the two cops. Jo led her to what looked to be the biggest living room she had ever seen. "I'm so sorry to have to tell you, but your husband's body was found early this morning."

"What? Where?"

"Over on Morningview Lane."

Melancon watched as shock registered on Mrs. Easterly's delicate face, "But what was he doing over there? We don't know anyone over there. Was he at a client's house?"

Melancon paid close attention to her facial expressions, "It looks as if his body was left there deliberately."

Mrs. Easterly let out a gasp, "He was murdered? But why would someone leave his body there?"

Melancon asked, "Do you know if your husband purchased some property to invest in or maybe rent?"

Mrs. Easterly shook her head, "As far as I know this is the only house we own. Are you sure it was Graham? I can't think of anyone that would want to murder him?"

Melancon took Mrs. Easterly's hand in hers, "Mrs. Easterly do you know Sheila Graves?"

"I know of her. I have seen her around town and maybe at a few functions, but I do not personally know her. Why?"

Melancon steadied herself because this would not be pleasant, "Your husband's body was left on Ms. Graves's doorstep. After doing some research, we have discovered that the house she lives in was purchased by your husband."

Melancon and Picou watched as the color drained from her face. Picou walked over to the bar and poured her a shot of scotch, "Here drink this. It will help calm your nerves."

Sandra Easterly took the drink from him, but just stared at Melancon, "I don't understand. Why would someone leave his body at her house? Why did he buy a house for a lady he didn't know?"

Melancon let her think about this for a few minutes before saying anything else. After a few minutes had passed, she asked, "Do you think it is possible your husband was having an affair?"

"What! No, he would not do that to me. Not after his last one. I told him if I caught him again, I would take every penny he has."

The next thing Melancon and Picou knew, Mrs. Easterly took the glass of scotch in her hands and threw it across the room, "That son of a bitch. He wasn't working late. He was screwing another woman. He wasn't too tired from work when he came home; he was too tired because he had been screwing some whore. I knew I should have cut his dick off the first time I caught him screwing around!"

Melancon knew she needed to tread carefully with this next question. This was a sensitive matter when dealing with domestic violence. She slowly picked up Mrs. Easterly's arm and carefully raised her shirt sleeve, "Mrs. Easterly did Graham do this to you?"

Mrs. Easterly snatched her hand away, "He gets angry sometimes, but he always apologizes afterwards. Besides, if I leave him where would I go? An affair would void our prenup, but who thought to put in a clause about abuse? My lawyer and I did not. The first time, and I thought the only time, he cheated on me I caught him. I reminded him what was in the prenup, and he begged me to give him another chance. He swore he would never do it again. He said it was just a one-time fling. He said he was weak, and she had tempted him. I should have known better. I should have listened to my therapist and left his ass."

Melancon asked, "Mrs. Easterly, who knew that Graham was hurting you?"

"The only person that knew was my therapist. He has been after me to leave Graham ever since I told him about the abuse. I just couldn't though. Graham always said he was sorry afterwards and bought me something nice to make up for it. He may leave a few inconspicuous bruises, but it was nothing like what I am sure you are used to dealing with. He made sure he never hit my face or did any serious damage. He mainly liked to slap me around. If it would have been worse, then I doubt I would have stayed with him, no matter the consequences."

Picou asked, "Has your husband mentioned anyone threatening him, maybe bothering him?"

She shook her head, "No, Graham may have done some rotten things for Devareaux, but he's never mentioned anyone attacking or threatening him personally. However, I do know there were plenty of people that hated the both of them. Graham let it all roll right off of him. He always said it was just business."

Melancon knew that there were people that hated both men, but she could not see someone here committing murder.

Mrs. Easterly looked at Melancon, "There won't be too many tears shed over either of these men's deaths. Graham may have had his faults, but no one deserves to be murdered."

Melancon kept her mouth closed. Mrs. Easterly didn't need to know just how horrific of a death her husband suffered. She also knew that the public might be worried that someone out there was killing members of this town. However, she didn't want to see them charging around town with a pitchfork waiting to find someone lurking in the shadows.

Mrs. Easterly asked, "What happens next?"

Melancon informed her, "Your husband's body is at the coroner's office. An autopsy will be performed to establish time and cause of death. We also need to confirm he was killed by the same person that killed Mrs. Russo and Mr. Devareaux."

Melancon handed her her business card, "Mrs. Easterly, again, I am sorry for your loss. Please call me if you have any questions."

Chapter 24

Mia was busy taking the beignet dough out of the refrigerator when Shelly came in. "Good morning Mia. I guess you heard about the excitement going around town."

Mia nodded, "I know they found another body."

Shelly looked at her in astonishment, "I still can't believe that Chad doesn't give you the full scoop. Girl, it is all over town that Graham Easterly was murdered. His body was found at Sheila Graves's house. Turns out, they have been having an affair for quite some time. I wonder if his wife knew about it."

Now this did shock Mia. She knew Sandra Easterly. Not only was she a beautiful woman, but she helped anyone in need. She thought Graham and Sandra were happy together. Sandra may be a recluse in some ways, but whenever she came into the bakery, she was always so kind.

"I can't believe that he was cheating on Sandra. Why on earth would he do that to her?"

Shelly shook her head, "I don't know, but the gossip mill is running full steam right now. I heard that Graham bought Sheila's house for her. I'm not sure how true that is though. You know how this town can be when they find out some dirt on you. Things tend to be blown out of proportion, but still it makes you wonder if there is some truth to it. I love Sheila to death, but I always wondered how she could afford such an extravagant house. I know she has the little gym here in town, but I didn't think it brought in that much."

Mia never stopped to think about the woman's financial situation. She didn't think it was any of her business, "I never thought about it to tell you the truth."

Shelly asked, "You don't think it's the same killer do you?"

Mia shook her head, "I sure hope not. It is kind of creepy though when you think about it. Three people killed here in town. I knew no one liked Devareaux, and some of the same people that hated Devareaux also hated Easterly. Easterly carried out most of Devareaux's dirty work after all."

Shelly agreed, "Yeah, but where does Victoria Russo fit into this? I knew her from high school, and I don't think she knew Devareaux or Easterly."

"I don't know. I think they may have run in the same social circles, but I don't believe they were friends."

Mia knew this was also puzzling Chad, but she did not say anything to Shelly. She didn't want to be the one spreading rumors. She'd had enough attention after Carl Ledet abducted her. She still was not sure how she walked away with her life. She thought she was a goner and would never see Chad or her family again. She was given a second chance at life and did not want to waste a second of it on gossip.

"I feel so sorry for Sandra. She will be the one to suffer because of Graham's disgusting behavior and the circus around his death."

Mia shook her head, "I can't imagine what the poor woman must be going through. I doubt they will release his body anytime soon. She will have to wait to bury him. I also look for them to question their friends to see who knew or suspected Graham was seeing Sheila."

Shelly told Mia, "Everyone is worried that this killer is trying to pick up where Carl Ledet left off."

Mia hoped there was not someone else as crazy as Carl Ledet lurking around this town. That man was depraved. She was glad he was dead. "I hope we don't have another person out there killing that is as crazy as Ledet. That is the last thing we need."

Shelly asked, "Have you heard if they have any suspects?"

Mia shook her head, "I don't know. I don't like asking Chad about police business. I have faith in him and Jo. If anyone can find this killer, it is those two. They discovered it was Ledet dumping those bodies in the bayou and rescued me just in time."

Shelly felt a shiver snake down her spine, "I just can't see someone from here doing something so vile. I heard Victoria's body was in awful shape. Who would want to hurt someone so bad?"

"I don't know. I grew up here and can't imagine anyone doing anything so horrible. However, I also grew up with Carl. I thought he was a little strange but never once imagined he could do what he did."

Mia hoped that Chad caught this killer soon. It may not bring back Victoria and the others, but maybe their souls would find peace in knowing their killer had been brought to justice.

Mia let out a groan when she saw LouAnn walk in the door. "LouAnn, you didn't have to bring the flowers over. I would have come by."

"I just couldn't stay away. I had to know if you heard about the latest murder victim. It was Graham Easterly. The whole town is buzzing about his murder and the scandal of it. I swear these men nowadays. First, we find out that Victoria Russo's husband had been cheating on her and now poor Sandra. She must be beside herself."

Shelly complained, "These men sure do seem to lead a double life."

"I just can't see how Sandra didn't know her husband had bought a house for that woman. I always thought of her as a smart woman. He must have controlled the money for him to set up a home for that bimbo of his. I thought Sheila was such a lovely young lady. You really don't know about people, do you?"

Mildred walked in and joined in on the gossip. "Mais, it's something about dis morning."

LouAnn smiled at her friend, "It is all everyone can talk about this morning. I tell you one thing, you won't find too many people offering sympathy for those two men."

Mia still hated that another person was dead, "I know people are bitter, but none of these people deserved to die the way they did."

Mildred shook her head, "Dere are some folks around here dat tink dey got what dey deserved, mais oui."

Mia let out an exasperated sigh, "Yeah, but it is the families of these victims that will pay in the long run. The whole town knows that Victoria Russo turned a blind eye to her husband's indiscretions. Now Sandra Easterly has to live with the fact that her husband has been cheating on her with a woman in the same town. Then the killer decided to leave the cheating husband's body at the mistress's front door. Both of these families have been humiliated in front of the whole town. This guy has not only murdered the victims, but he is punishing the families."

LouAnn mulled this over, "I don't think the killer thought about the families to be honest with you. I think his primary concern is showing that these people were committing sins right under everyone's nose."

Mia asked, "Yeah, but who knows what goes on behind closed doors? I mean with Eric Devareaux that was easy, but I don't think anyone in town knew what went on at the Russo or Easterly house."

Mildred let out a gasp, "Mais I never taught about dat."

Chapter 25

On the drive home, Jo wondered what other secrets would be revealed during these murder investigations. She had learned more dirty little secrets about the members of this town than she cared to know. This was turning into their own little soap opera with all the adultery and drama.

She wondered whose secrets would be revealed next. It was only a matter of time before the killer struck again. He was not even waiting two weeks in between murders. He was using the seven deadly sins for his murdering spree, but then what happened? Would he stop killing? She knew in her gut that was unlikely.

Jo had barely made it home when her doorbell rang. Looking through the peephole, she had to suppress a smile. She opened the door to let Bill in, "I promise you I was going to give you a call. I just made it home."

Bill held up a bag, "I come bearing gifts. I figured you didn't have a chance to eat today."

Jo's mouth was watering just from the tempting aromas, "That smells like jambalaya from Cherie's."

He held his other hand up and showed her the beers, "It is. I also picked up a six pack while I was there."

"I may have to find a way to thank you."

Bill looked at her and winked, "We may be able to come to an agreeable payment."

Jo laughed as she closed the door. "Do you want to make ourselves comfortable in the living room or would you prefer to eat in the dining room?"

"I'm sure you had one of those days where you want to kick off your shoes and relax. Let's go into the living room. I have to get the story to the editor by midnight."

"Well, let's eat and we can talk about the case."

Jo grabbed some silverware and paper towels from the kitchen before heading to the living room. By the time she made it in there, Bill had the plates and beer laid out on the coffee table.

"Ladies first."

Jo picked up a plate and made herself comfortable on the sofa. She was surprised when Bill sat down next to her. She figured he would choose one of the recliners. "This hits the spot. Thank you so much."

"It's the least I could do considering I am getting ready to pump you for information."

Jo smiled over at him, "For jambalaya pump away." She took a forkful of the chicken and sausage rice mixture, savoring its Cajun spiciness. She let out a moan in pleasure. "This is so good."

Bill took a bite from his plate, "I have to admit it is good. I was half afraid it would be the tomato based one I grew up with."

"Mais non, Pierre he knows how to cook true Cajun food."

Bill let his curiosity take over, "So now that there has been a third murder, do you think that Bear Corner has another serial killer?"

"I think we have a killer with a set mission. I hate to say the words serial killer and get the public anxious, but all three people were definitely killed by the same person."

"But don't you think the public needs to be concerned?"

"We haven't even found the connection between Victoria Russo and the other two victims. It's obvious both men were well hated individuals in the community."

Bill nodded in agreement, "True. But this killer has struck three times in less than six weeks. He isn't giving himself much down time."

Jo shook her head, "No, Chad and I are not sure how much longer before he strikes again. He is not keeping to a set schedule." Sighing, "You can feel the tension growing around town. Everyone is getting scared. I don't think we should start jumping at shadows just yet. Whoever this is knew that Graham Easterly was cheating on his wife. Not many people knew that bit of information. That helps shorten our suspect list. I just don't want to feed the public information that will create a mass panic."

Bill contemplated everything she said, "So exactly what do you want me to print?"

"All I am asking is that you be responsible. There is a very thin line here that can be easily crossed where people begin shooting at things that go bump in the night."

Bill asked, "So you want me to hold off on saying that there is an actual serial killer out there?"

"What I do know is that we have three murders committed by the same individual. I know this criteria fits for a serial killer, but I hate to use those exact words."

"So basically we have a lunatic hunting people he believes have done something wrong. It would be easier if these killers didn't look like you and me, if they wore horns or showed their real inner self."

Jo let out a sigh, "Tell me about it. It sure would make my job easier. I just want you to be careful in how you word this. We don't need everyone in town freaking out just yet."

"Have y'all considered inviting in the FBI?"

Jo shook her head, "At this point there is no need to ask them. They have their hands full with more demented killers than we are looking for. Besides, this isn't something that would interest them just yet. Our perp has killed three local people. Usually, the FBI asks for a different demographic before they step in. Besides, we have an excellent police force here, along with exceptional labs and a damn fine medical examiner."

Bill put his hands up as if to surrender, "Point taken detective. I didn't mean to make it sound like y'all can't handle the case. I was just asking."

As they talked, they seemed to touch accidentally. They were innocent little touches, nothing offensive. He draped his arm casually around her shoulders after they finished eating as they sat there and talked. Even sitting this close together, she had no sense of her personal space being invaded; it felt natural to have him sitting right beside her. When he leaned over and kissed her, she thought for sure time stood still.

Bill stood up and pulled her up from the couch. Jo's breath caught; she had been dreaming of this moment. He kissed her one more time. "I got to go. I have a deadline to make, and I know you need to get a good night's sleep."

Jo thought the kiss would lead to something more. "You're sure you can't stay a little longer?"

"No, I need to get my piece in before my editor starts raising hell."

She tried to hide her disappointment that he wasn't staying, "I guess you're right. I do need to get some sleep so that I can have a fresh start in the morning. I want to nail this bastard to the wall."

"I have complete faith in you. You are a damn good detective."

"Yeah, well, being a woman detective isn't easy in this line of business. You have to prove yourself constantly. Don't get me wrong, Detective Picou and Sheriff Riley are great, but some officers don't believe a woman should be a cop."

On her way to the office the following morning, Jo thought about what happened, or didn't happen, last night with Bill. She was disappointed the kiss with him didn't lead to more. Still, she wanted to know the man a little more. She sensed that there was more to him than he let on, and it was part of her instinct to dig until she found out everything there was to know. He wasn't making it easy for her though.

Maybe the unknown was part of the attraction she felt for him. That and the way he made her feel. She couldn't seem to get enough of him.

Chapter 26

Sheriff Riley looked up from his desk and tried to hide a scowl. Mayor Daigle was walking towards his office, not bothering to check in with the receptionist. Damn, why didn't he shut his door?

He didn't understand why the man couldn't just pick up the phone to check in. Mais non, he had to drop by with no warning.

Mayor Daigle walked into his office, "Sheriff, do you have any more information about these murders?" he asked without preamble.

Before Sheriff Riley could stand up, Mayor Daigle sank into one of the visitor's chairs and reached for one of the files on Riley's desk. *Mon Dieu, of all the nerve.*

Riley tried to stack the files neatly in front of him, "Nothing that you don't already know sir. I wish you would have called before heading over here, I could have saved you the trip."

He watched as Mayor Daigle shrugged his shoulders, "I had planned on coming over this way anyhow. I wanted to check on the progress of this case personally. My phone is ringing off the hook with worried constituents wanting answers. I want this man stopped before he can kill again."

Sheriff Riley stiffened at the tone, "Sir, with all due respect we are working this case the best way we can. This list of enemies Devareaux and Easterly had is over a mile long. I have deputies working overtime trying to round up everyone's alibis. It is a slow process, but we are making headway. The list of potential suspects dwindles with each person's confirmed alibi."

"Are we dealing with the same killer at least?"

Sheriff Riley looked him in the eye, "Without a doubt, sir. I have asked that no one use the term serial killer, especially when talking with the press, but they were all killed by the same person."

"Do you think we need to consider bringing in the big guns?"

Sheriff Riley shook his head, "No sir. This isn't something they would be interested in right now. Besides, no outsider is going to know the people in this town better than our own. We will put the pieces together and find this killer. Unfortunately, we are looking for someone local who is committing these murders.

"My primary concern right now is I don't want the word serial killer leaked to the press, especially after Carl Ledet. We don't need to put this town into a panic."

"People are already getting scared. I can hear it in their voices every time they call."

Sheriff Riley informed him, "They may be scared, but no one is panicking. Right now, everyone in town believes that Devareaux and Easterly pissed off the wrong person and that somehow Victoria Russo was caught in the middle. I don't think anyone has connected the dots, and I want to keep it that way."

"And what do you propose I tell these concerned citizens?"

Sheriff Riley tried to keep the irritation out of his voice, "You can tell them Bear Corner's finest are diligently working on catching this killer. Ask them to please keep their doors and windows locked at night, be careful, and pay attention to their surroundings." He left out the part that they should all mind their own business. There was no need to ruffle feathers any more than they already were.

Sheriff Riley ran a hand through his hair, "Look, sir, I know this is frustrating, but we really are doing our job. These people are busting their asses to get this case solved. They stay late and come in early. The budget for overtime pay has gone out the window. Every man is working on this investigation. Everyone in this department wants to catch this killer. We are doing the very best we can."

"Yet you still don't have a suspect for even one of the murders?"

Riley let out an exasperated sigh, "No, sir, not yet."

"You don't need me telling you how to do your job, but I want this killer stopped, and it's not just me. Judging from the phone calls my office has been getting, the citizens of Bear Corner also want to see some results. We can't afford any mistakes. I don't want this guy walking so make sure you get solid evidence when you bring in someone. I have no desire to see a guilty person walk away on a technicality."

"You won't have to sir, I know my job."

Mayor Daigle stood up from his chair, "Keep me advised would you? The town council is on my case. I don't want it to appear to anyone that y'all are sitting on your hands. We sure as hell don't need someone saying the murders weren't looked into because it was felt these people deserved to die."

"Sir, no one deserves to die the way these victims did. Their murders were gruesome."

Relief washed over Sheriff Riley as he watched Mayor Daigle walk out of the office. He had no doubt the man would be back here soon.

Chapter 27
Gluttony

Brian LeBlanc loved food. It was the one thing he couldn't get enough of. He had tried memberships to the local gyms, but it was useless. He was not morbidly obese, but he was overweight. His personality helped make up for his physical appearance. He was smart, adventurous and a friendly person. People liked him.

His job as a local food critic for The Tribune was ideal for him. Being on the payroll to sample various foods was perfect for him. He dined at classy, upscale restaurants. Eating delicious food was such an experience.

Whenever Brian was at a restaurant, he never took notes. That would take away from his experience. When he returned to his car he would write down every significant detail, reveling in the tastes and textures of the food all over again.

Eating was more about savoring the good food, learning its textures and nuances. He enjoyed delicious food. He liked the gourmet side of food. Once you had a gourmet, high class, properly prepared meal you would understand what he meant.

As Brian stepped out of the restaurant, the humid Louisiana night air slapped him in the face. The air was cloying, damp, and sticky. The heat was oppressive. A few cars were still out on the road. The smell of the bayou was heavy. Streetlights offered little illumination to this dark night.

Thick, dark clouds promising rain blocked the moonlight. He greeted a few people as he headed to his car.

***

As he watched the sinner make his way to his car he wondered how many more of these people were sinners as well. Who else needed to repent for their sins?

He watched as Brian left his latest feast. He breathed in the heady scent of the dark, insidious aroma of the bayou.

 He turned on the radio and let the soothing voice of the person reciting the Rosary fill the air. The Rosary reciting in the background helped calm him for his mission.

This man should be ashamed of himself. Gluttony was thought to be an over indulgence of food. Gluttony, however, was the consumption of anything in excess. That was what made it one of the seven deadly sins.

He could clearly see that Brian put food above all else. He wrote about it as a living. His writing talent should be used for something more worthwhile.

***

As Brian walked into his house, he swore he was in the presence of evil. A deep, primal fear sent a chill down his body. He attempted to shake off the eerie feeling.

Even though he was safe in his home, he still felt exposed. It was as if someone or something was watching his every move. With an uneasy knot in the pit of his stomach, he checked to make sure all the doors and windows were locked.

He grabbed a snack of Brie, figs and wafer crackers along with a glass of Moscato to take to bed. He wanted to finish writing his review before falling asleep. He could still taste the Chicken Marsala he had for supper tonight. The moment it hit his tongue, his taste buds came to life. The white chocolate cheesecake with fresh strawberry glaze was pure heaven. It melted in his mouth. It was so light on his lips, absolutely delicious. Nothing, though, could compare to Mia Picou's Pistachio Cake with White Chocolate Buttercream. He had been meaning to order a whole cake just for himself. He needed to set a reminder to do that in the morning. He suspected the dessert from tonight's restaurant came from there. That woman could work miracles with desserts. He wished he lived next door to her bakery. He would be in there from the time they opened until they closed. Just thinking of the wondrous concoctions she whipped up sent him into a sweet abyss.

He had just fallen asleep when a noise woke him up with a start. He bolted upright. He glanced around the room in a panic, trying to see what woke him up. The moonlight filtered through the curtains, illuminating the room in a soft glow.

Brian felt a jolt of electricity travel through his body. Everything went hazy and he blacked out.

A cramp in Brian's arm woke him. He went to work it out and fear washed over him. He couldn't move his arms. He tried to kick the covers off him and realized he couldn't move his arms or legs. He quickly opened his eyes, but all he saw was darkness.

He heard footsteps and terror began to take over his body.

***

He heard his sinner waking up and headed to the table. As he looked down at the man who needed to atone for his sins, he picked up the knife.

He turned on the overhead light and informed his captive. "You must atone for your sins."

He struggled against the restraints. The restraints on his wrists and ankles were secured tightly. There was no chance of escaping.

***

He didn't know what this man meant by atoning for his sins. Was this guy some kind of religious freak that believed he could save his soul? "I don't know what sins you are talking about?"

He cringed as the knife skimmed over his body. White-hot pain seared through his body as the knife was thrust deep into his flesh. Tears blurred his vision. He screamed out in pain as his captor cut him again.

He slashed at his body repeatedly. The pain was excruciating. He begged God for death to come quickly.

***

He watched as the life faded from the sinner's eyes. He recited, "Dominus vobiscum."

It was pitch black outside still. He knew exactly where to display the body. It was time for the town to see this man's sins.

Chapter 28

Picou walked into the house to find Mia busy in the kitchen. "Mais, it is a mess in here."

Mia threw a rag at him, "Oh you! I am trying to make crepes. I want to add something new to the menu."

Chad looked around the kitchen, "I think you have enough crepes here to feed an army."

Mia shook her head, "But they still aren't right yet."

Chad bit into one and moaned in delight, "I don't know, they taste like perfection to me."

Chad grabbed himself a cup of coffee and a plate. He helped himself to a couple more of the crepes Mia had been busy making, "I can't decide which ones I like best."

"You sure you aren't just saying that since you sleep with me."

"Mais non. I'm going to have to work off all these extra calories." He looked over at her and winked, "Now to figure out how. Do you have any ideas?"

Mia walked over to him and licked off some of the filling left behind on his lips, "I guess we can go for a walk tonight."

Chad swatted her on her behind, "Is that how you want to work these calories off, a walk?"

She snuggled into him a little more, "I may be able to think of a few other ways."

Chapter 29

Detective Jo Melancon had finished her morning run and was anxious to jump in a cool shower when her phone rang. She let out a groan when she noticed it was the dispatcher calling, "Melancon."

"Detective we got another body."

So much for a long shower, "Where is it?"

"It is at Pierre's."

She informed the dispatcher, "I'm on my way. Have you called Detective Picou yet?"

"Mia is the one that found the body so she called him first thing. He asked that I call you."

Jo felt sorry for poor Mia. This was the last thing Mia wanted to deal with right now. As she drove to the crime scene, her phone rang once again. It was Picou, "Damn man, I'm on my way."

"Get your ass in gear woman. This guy is escalating. There was a lot of mutilation done to this man's body."

By the time she reached the crime scene, it looked like a full-blown circus. Not only had a crowd of bystanders shown up, but also the media were crawling all over the place. They were all trying to catch a glimpse of the dead body. *Great, just what they needed - more media coverage.* It wouldn't be long before this case went national and when it did, everyone would be looking over their shoulder.

She found Picou near the body. He was quiet, just staring down at the deceased. She let him collect his thoughts. She winced when she saw the remains. The carnage was brutal.

He showed her the note, "Brian LeBlanc must repent for GLUTTONY."

He informed her, "I believe our guy has snapped. This is another dumpsite. We still have no idea where he is murdering these victims. All we can do is pray that he messed up and left some evidence behind."

Sheriff Riley watched as the medical examiner's office zipped up the body bag. His lifeless eyes showed the horror he went through hours before. If only the dead could tell them who did this.

Melancon walked up beside him, "I just don't understand this. Brian wasn't even in the same social circles as the previous victims. Brian is, or was, so sweet. Everyone loved him. I can't picture him being guilty of gluttony. He never seemed to over indulge in food."

Sheriff Riley shook his head, "I just don't understand this guy. What connects all these victims? There has to be a something that we aren't seeing. We need to find it fast."

Melancon looked over the crime scene again, "There is always a chance this killer is choosing his victims randomly."

Sheriff Riley pursed his lips, "Maybe, but I have a gut feeling that something ties all these victims together. This serial killer has a rage specific to these victims. This unsub is probably stalking his victims for a while. He gets to know their routines before moving in to strike. These were premeditated murders. He drugs them beforehand. He wants complete control of his victims so that he can torture them. They may even know the killer. There have been no defensive wounds on the victims. He also wants these bodies found. He takes great pride in the display. He wants the shock value."

Melancon added, "I have a feeling he drugs these victims to render them helpless so that he can unload his grievances. He gives them just enough to control them, but he needs them to understand why they are being punished. He wants these people to pay for their sins."

Picou agreed, "But how did he know that they were even guilty of these sins?"

Melancon shrugged her shoulders, "That is what we need to find out. I've been compiling a list, but now with Brian thrown into the mix none of this makes sense."

Picou stated, "A local is doing this. He is definitely stalking these victims beforehand. A stranger would be noticed skulking about at night for any reason. No, our killer knows this area and knows that no one will question why he was out and about."

Melancon looked around the crime scene. The crowd of onlookers was growing by the minute. She guessed it was just human nature to be curious, but she wondered if someone in the crowd was the killer.

Chapter 30

Mia stepped into the shower and let the hot water beat down on her. She adjusted the showerhead to pulsate. The pounding water against her scalp helped force out the images of Brian LeBlanc's mutilated body. Every time she closed her eyes, she saw the garish sight.

The cold seemed to penetrate straight to her bones. Even with the heat from the water wrapping its steamy arms around her, she could not get the image of death out of her mind, no matter how hard she tried. She wished she could doze off into a sweet oblivion for a while but she knew sleep would elude her for a while tonight.

Mia stepped out of the shower and dressed. She walked into her kitchen and pulled out everything for supper. Maybe cooking would help ease her mind.

***

Picou stood up from his desk to stretch his back. He had been looking at the computer screen for hours trying to find a connection between the murder victims. Other than the note stating their sin, he could find none.

His stomach let out a loud rumble reminding him that he hadn't eaten since breakfast. He looked down at his watch to see what time it was and was surprised to see that it was already after seven o'clock. Mon Dieu, he had been at this longer than he realized.

His cell phone rang and he cringed. He was almost afraid to see who it was. A smile formed on his face when he saw it was Mia, "Cher, I'm so glad it is you calling."

"I was just calling to see if you wanted me to bring you supper. I have crawfish etouffee with homemade French bread."

Picou's mouth watered at the thought of her etouffee. "I am turning off my computer as we speak and heading home."

"It's no problem if you want me to bring it over there. I know you have your hands full with these murders right now."

"Until Brian LeBlanc's death the general public was worried, but some felt that Devareaux and Easterly deserved what they got. Now there is a public outcry for this killer to be stopped."

"That is all everyone talks about in the bakery nowadays. Poor Victoria Russo's death seems to have been forgotten." Sighing, "Are you sure you don't want me to bring you supper?"

"Mais non, I need a break. The media is crawling all over the place. I hate to see you push your way through them. Besides, they may smell your good cooking and try to tackle you for it."

Mia let out a soft laugh, "I'll be waiting for you."

"Are you holding up okay cher?"

"I've been cooking up a storm. You will be bringing in all kinds of goodies to the office tomorrow. Every time I close my eyes, I see Brian's body. Who would do this to him? He was such a nice man."

"I don't know cher, but I am looking for him."

Chapter 31

Before heading home, Jo called Bill. "Did you want to meet to discuss the case, or would you rather do this over the phone?"

"I better get what you have over the phone tonight. It is late and I have been busy writing up a story from what I already know."

Jo wondered how he obtained some of his information so early on in the investigation. He was probably going off the rumors that were spreading around town. She had hoped he would want to meet in person. She wanted to know more about him. For some reason he was a closed book. Maybe it was the fact that he was a journalist and they generally tended to keep secrets, only revealing them when it was necessary.

Jo informed him, "Why don't you ask what you are curious about, and then I will help fill in the blanks with what I can release?"

"That'll work, but when this is done, I want an exclusive interview with the fabulous detective that captured this elusive killer."

Jo let out a laugh, "Thanks for the boost of confidence tonight. I really needed it."

Jo swore she could hear him smiling over the phone. "Not a problem. Who said chivalry was dead? Anyway, back to the case – Is it true that Mia found the body?"

"Off the record, Mia did find the body, but Chad is not going to allow anyone near her for an interview."

Bill let out a sigh, "Fair enough I guess. I can see where he would want to protect her, but still it won't be long before the bakery is flooded with reporters wanting to talk to her."

"I'll let Chad and Mia know that you want to talk to her. That is all I can do for you on that matter. The ball will be in their court."

"I guess I will have to live with that for now. Is it true that the deceased was the food critic Brian LeBlanc?"

"Next of kin has been notified so I can confirm that the murder victim was Brian LeBlanc."

Bill let out a whistle, "Man, I can't see this guy being killed by this maniac. From what I knew about Brian, everyone loved him. I don't think he had any enemies at the paper."

Jo agreed, "No, from everyone I have talked with so far he had no enemies and we still have no connection to him and the other victims."

"So you are no closer to a suspect at this time."

Jo shook her head and then realized he couldn't see her over the phone, "No, we still have no viable suspects."

"So, basically you are at the same place in the investigation as you were the previous day except that you have another murder victim."

Jo agreed with Bill, "That's it in a nutshell. As soon as I have something further to give you I promise I will let you know."

Bill ended the conversation, "I will have to bring you supper one of these days, but tonight I need to get this story written."

"And I need to try and get some sleep. Good night Bill."

"Good night Jo. I hope you have sweet dreams tonight."

After hanging up with Bill, Jo wondered if she would be able to sleep or if it would elude her once again. Before leaving the office, Jo had done some research on the various serial killers out there and she believed theirs was a mission-oriented killer. He was out to eliminate a particular group he felt unworthy of living.

Unfortunately, their serial killer also fit the profile of a visionary killer. She wondered if he was killing these "sinners" because he believed God was telling him to do so. Either way, she speculated about what the stressor in his life was that made him decide to begin killing.

Chapter 32

Mia had decided after Brian LeBlanc's body was found next door to the bakery she would close for the day. The cops had the area cordoned off anyway, so no one would be able to get near the place. Besides, she didn't feel like answering a bunch of questions so soon after finding the body.

She knew she couldn't afford two days of being closed, so the next morning she planned to be there earlier than usual to prep for the day. Mia had a feeling that it would be busy today with customers and those who wanted to stop by and gossip. She said a quick prayer asking God to give her the strength to deal with the busybodies.

When Shelly arrived the following day, Mia had an assortment of crepes prepared. The beignets were ready to fry and an assortment of goodies awaited the customers. It was an hour before they were to open and she noticed a crowd growing out front. Not wanting to have them continue waiting, she opened early.

She walked over and moved the sign to "open" and greeted the crowd, "Y'all may as well come in and get it while it's hot. We have a few new things on the menu that I want honest opinions on."

LouAnn came over and gave Mia a hug, "Cher how are you holding up?"

"Mais, I am doing okay. It was a shock yesterday, though."

"Mais oui. I couldn't believe it when I heard the news. I talked to Chad for a few minutes while he was out here and he said that you had gone home. I wanted to go see you, but he suggested that I let you be for a little while, that you were upset over finding the body.”

Mia would have to thank Chad later on. She had no idea he had saved her from the harpies. “I don’t know if I can ever erase that image from my mind. I don’t know how Chad deals with death day in and day out.”

“Mais, he has you to come home to, that’s how. He is a lucky man.”

Mia let out a laugh, “You may be right.”

“Of course I’m right. I tell you these murders are getting out of hand. Brian LeBlanc has never done anybody wrong.”

“Brian’s death was surprising. There seems to be no rhyme or reason to the killings.”

“Mon Dieu, we may all be at risk. Does that man of yours have any leads as to who is doing this? I just can’t believe that it is someone from here.”

“Chad hasn’t said anything. I know they are working around the clock to find out who is doing this.”

“I don’t see how Brian is connected to the other victims. Especially those two snakes in the grass, Devareaux and Easterly. You would think Sheriff Riley would make a statement to the public to help put our mind at ease.”

Mia informed LouAnn, “I know they are working hand in hand with The Tribune to keep everyone up to date on what is happening, but I don't see them releasing information that is fundamental to the actual investigation."

Mia watched as Mildred walked into the bakery and headed over to them, "Good morning Mildred."

"Mornin' cher. How are you doing dis morning?"

"I'm doing better."

"Dese killings make me moitie fou."

LouAnn hugged her friend, "This latest killing is making us all half crazy with fear. And we have no idea who the killer may go after next. Mia and I were just talking about how Brian LeBlanc was such a good man. He just doesn't tie in with the other victims, mais non."

Mia noticed the bakery was filling up, "As much as I would love to stay and continue our visit, I need to get back into the kitchen and get some more beignets out."

Mildred gave Mia a hug, "Un jour a la fois."

Mia hugged her back, "I'm trying to take it one day at a time."

Mildred told her, "Dis was da reason I didn't want to live in da big city, but now da violence is here too."

Mia let out a sigh when she was back in the kitchen. As much as she loved those two women, they sure could gossip up a storm. These four murders had the town in turmoil and Mia feared that no one was safe from this killer's wrath.

Chapter 33

Sheriff Riley walked into his office and shut his door. This last murder had turned the town upside down. The phones had been ringing nonstop since yesterday morning.

He just couldn't see the connection between Brian LeBlanc and the previous victims. What were they missing? What connected these victims? Was it just something in the killer's mind?

Feeling restless about this case, he left his office and went over to the conference room where Detectives Picou and Melancon were hard at work on this case. They had previously set up a murder board and laid out the cases to search for clues that they may have missed.

Melancon looked up from the file, "Morning, Sheriff."

"How is it going?"

Melancon let out an exasperated sigh, "Mon Dieu, we have gone over everything with a fine tooth comb, but nothing links these victims together besides the fact that the killer believed they have sinned."

Sheriff Riley scowled deeply as he stared at the boards, "But how in the hell was Brian LeBlanc guilty of gluttony? Everyone I have talked to was shocked about his murder. Unlike the others no one had anything bad to say about him."

Melancon shrugged her shoulders, "That is why we are beating our heads against the brick wall. We are digging into his personal life the best we can, but so far we have come up empty handed."

Sheriff Riley ran his hands through his hair, "This killer found out something about Brian LeBlanc that set him off. Dig deeper! There is something there. We just have to find it."

Sheriff Riley walked over to the window and stared outside. He watched as people came and went from the courthouse and other businesses that made up downtown. The vendors were busy setting up for the lunch crowd. The killer was out there. Could one of these people be the killer? If so, what had suddenly set them off?

He turned back to Melancon, "We need to dig deeper into any newcomers. There haven't been too many people who moved here in the last year or so."

Melancon started taking notes, "I will have the computer techs get right on that. I can also have them run the names against those that had a personal grudge against Devareaux and Easterly just in case the other murders were to throw us off the trail."

Sheriff Riley asked Picou, "What about witnesses? No one has noticed anything out of the ordinary?"

Picou admitted begrudgingly, "So far we haven't been able to find any. No one noticed anything out of the ordinary that day or the days leading up to the murder. Hell, no one even noticed anything when the bodies were disposed of. It's almost as if this guy is a ghost."

He watched as the sheriff's scowl deepened further, "Somehow this killer is finding out what these victims' sins are. We have to figure out how he is learning the details of these victims' lives. He knows more than even their spouses knew."

Picou groaned, "Right now we are playing a waiting game and I hate waiting."

Sheriff Riley half nodded in agreement, "The killer is the one in control, and I want to switch roles with him. We have to wait for the other shoe to drop. It is completely unnerving."

"If I'm correct in my analogy and he is going by the seven deadly sins, then there are three more potential victims out there. I wish we had a way of knowing when, where and who is next. So far, we haven't found a single person that had a grudge against these victims. Granted, we are still sifting through their lives.   These people kept their secrets well hidden so whoever did this was privy to the most intimate details of their lives."

Sheriff Riley wondered, "Maybe we are wasting time combing through the victims' lives. Maybe we need to trace their movements over the last week or two before their deaths. Maybe they crossed paths with the killer."

"I'll organize some officers to track the victims' movements and see if maybe we find a common denominator that way. You know this will add up to more overtime."

Sheriff Riley nodded, "Just do it. I want this bastard behind bars where he belongs."

Sheriff Riley noticed how tired Picou looked. Hell, they all looked as if they needed a good night's sleep, but that would have to wait until the case was closed.

Picou suggested, "I still don't think these victims did anything personally to this killer. With the staging of the bodies I believe he meant for the town to know these individuals were guilty of a sin."

"But how did this guy find out about their secret lives? He is leaving us virtually no trail to follow and with no evidence we have almost no chance of catching him, unless he makes a mistake."

Picou eyed him somewhat grimly, "I don't see our guy making a mistake."

"Realistically, neither do I. I also don't like that he changed his MO with Devareaux."

Picou informed him, "That was because the only way he could get close to Devareaux was by drugging his alcohol. His security was so tight around that house that a mouse could set it off. Only the killer didn't know that if the alarm system was tripped it only alerted Devareaux and not the police. If our killer had known that, then Devareaux's murder would have been messier."

Sheriff Riley sighed, "It could be this guy was just playing with us too, and wanted to throw us off the trail."

"If that was the case, then he wouldn't have left us the note. No, he wanted us to know that Devareux was a sinner, but hell just about everyone in town knew the greedy bastard only cared about money and how to get his hands on even more.

Sheriff Riley nodded his head in agreement, "I agree that this killer has a game plan all laid out. Now to figure out what it is."

Chapter 34

Picou had the reports and crime scene pictures spread out in front of him. The more he looked at the grisly crime scenes the more disgusted he became. What could drive a person to commit these heinous crimes, but more importantly, who knew that these victims were committing these sins?

Picou had been studying the seven deadly sins to see how they could fit into the killer's beliefs. Russo's note had pride written on it. Her friends had confirmed that she loved spending money and showing off her wealth. None of her friends knew that her husband was cheating on her, but they all agreed that she would turn the other cheek and keep spending his money. She was very proud of her body and her wealth. Devareaux's note had greed on it and everyone knew how greedy he was. Since Mrs. Easterly confirmed that her husband "slapped her around", they could confirm the wrath note left on Graham Easterly's body.

Brian LeBlanc's murder was the wrench in his theory, even with the gluttony note left behind. Brian was a top food critic and his house did have various foods in it, but there was no way he could be considered an overweight person. His stomach contents were full of food though. They weren't sure if he was gluttonous of food or if there was something more. Picou ran his hands through his hair as he studied a little more on the deadly sin of gluttony. Maybe there was a side to Brian that they didn't know. The man was pleasant and always had a smile on his face. Picou had only known him a short while, but he always seemed to be upbeat. He would keep digging into Brian's personal life, but in parenthesis, he jotted down gluttonous of what.

The next question to answer was who knew that Victoria Russo turned a blind eye to her husband's infidelities, that Graham Easterly beat his wife, and that Brian LeBlanc secretly gorged himself on rich foods? He did not recall hearing rumors and with this being a small town any little indiscretion spread like wildfire.

He let out a yawn and looked at his wristwatch. Damn, it was after eleven o'clock. His stomach let out a loud growl; he had not eaten since lunchtime. He wondered what Mia cooked for supper. He thought about calling her, but decided against it. She was probably fast asleep since she had to be up early in the morning. This case had prevented him from spending any quality time with her. He was about to get up when he felt someone massage his shoulders. Surprised, he looked up to see Mia smiling down at him, "I figured if I wanted to see you I better come to the Sheriff's Office. I wanted to wait until later, though, when I figured the media would have left for the day. Besides, I thought you could use a break."

Picou stood up, pulled her into his arms, and gave her a kiss. He breathed in her scent. She always smelled so intoxicating. She reminded him of a steamy southern night, a light floral mix of magnolia, jasmine, and gardenia. "I was getting ready to call it a day when you came in."

Mia picked up the basket of goodies, "So do you want to eat here?"

He eyed the basket, "Do you have more at home?"

She looked at him skeptically, "I have a little more left at the house, why?"

"Let's leave it for the night dispatcher. I'm sure he would appreciate a good meal. I can warm up something when I get home."

Mia shrugged her shoulders, "That's fine with me. I can make you a hot ham and Swiss cheese sandwich if you'd rather."

He took the basket from her and leaned down to kiss her, "Anything you make is bound to be good, but if my nose is right then this smells like your jambalaya."

She grinned, "It is, but this time I tried something different and used boiled shrimp."

"Well, let's get home. My mouth is watering already."

She looked around at the mess on the table, "Did you at least get anywhere?"

He shook his head, "No. We can't figure out how he is choosing these victims."

"Maybe you are trying too hard. I may know just the thing to take your mind off of the case for a while."

He draped an arm around her as they left, "And just what might that be?"

"Get me home and find out."

***

As Mia followed Chad home, she thought about how perfect her life was right now. She had never been happier.

Chapter 35
Sloth

Pam Benoit eased herself onto the chaise lounge in the great room. She picked up the remote to see what was on. She heard the housekeeper picking up in the kitchen and was annoyed that she could hear her working. Why must she always make so much noise when she was ready to sit down and watch TV?

She heard footsteps approaching behind her, "Ma'am, can I get you anything from the kitchen before I finish cleaning?"

"That would be great. I would love another cup of coffee."

"As you wish, ma'am." She knew her employer would never get up from her lounge to fix herself anything. She had never met a lazier person. If her butt was not parked in front of the TV then it was in front of that computer screen. The housekeeper doubted her employer had ever broken a true sweat ever in her lifetime.

The housekeeper brought out a tray with a cup of fresh coffee and lemon squares. As soon as she put down the tray, the doorbell rang.

"Get that, please?"

Rolling her eyes behind her employer's back, "Yes, ma'am."

"It's probably the man I hired to paint the guest room for me. Would you show him where it is? David should have everything in there for him."

"Yes, ma'am."

The painter stopped in the room to make sure the she had no further instructions, "I'm getting ready to start ma'am. Did you have any specific instructions?"

"Make sure you are finished today. I don't want you milking my husband for more money."

"Yes, ma'am, I will be finished today. It will need a day to dry though."

"Good, good. Get started then, stop dawdling."

***

Something about the painter gave the housekeeper the creeps. She planned to stay out of his way. He had his ball cap pulled down low and when she talked to him; he wouldn't look her in the eyes.

Lord knew if her employer couldn't get up to answer the door there was no way she would bother painting a simple room. If company wasn't arriving tonight and she wanted the house perfect, the housekeeper had a feeling she would be painting the room.

The housekeeper kept an eye on him as he brought in his supplies. Mais non, she didn't trust him one bit. He looked around as if he was memorizing every detail. He was probably casing the place out to rob it blind.

***

He heard the housekeeper tell Pam that she had to run to the store to get everything for supper. He should have known someone as lazy as her would have a housekeeper. Heaven forbid that she should lift a finger to do anything.

While the housekeeper was gone, he acted quickly. He picked up the ketamine soaked rag and headed over to the sleeping woman. She never woke up when he walked up behind her. He clamped the rag over her mouth and nose, letting her breath it in as she slept. She never even stirred.

Looking outside to make sure no one was around; he loaded her up into the van and headed back to his house.

As he looked down at the woman who needed to atone for her sins, he ran the tip of the blade against his tongue, drawing blood. The metallic flavor fueled his desire and quickened his movements.

She was guilty of sloth. Sloth was a laziness of the body and apathy of the soul. Occasionally, everyone enjoyed a lazy day, but true sloth was one of the deadly sins. When their morality went soft, they manipulated others to carry their weight. Sloth could take many guises; Pam Benoit had no discernible purpose in life. She enjoyed a lavish self-indulgent lifestyle.

He looked at her, "You must atone for your sins."

***

Pam whimpered as she struggled against the restraints. Her wrists and ankles were secured tightly to the table. She could not understand why he was doing this to her.

She didn't know what he meant by atoning for her sins. Was he a religious freak that believed he could save her soul?

She pulled against the restraints again and he laughed at her futile attempts. She cringed as he ran the knife over her naked body.

She shuddered in fear as he contemplated his next move. "Please, I'm begging you," she implored, "let me go. I won't tell anybody."

He chuckled softly as she felt the knife cutting into her body. Excruciating pain seared through her. Tears blurred her vision. Her reaction was instantaneous and she squirmed, trying to free herself from the restraints. She screamed out in pain.

She cried out as the knife cut into her once again. She writhed against the restraints, but he didn't stop the torment. He slashed her repeatedly.

The pain was agonizing, all consuming. Tears streamed down her face. She begged God for forgiveness, praying death came swiftly.

She felt her flesh ripping, her body being torn apart. The strange thing about this whole matter was she no longer felt any pain. Could it be that she had reached such a level of pain that her body no longer registered it or maybe her nerves were so damaged by the viciousness of this attack that the signals no longer reached her brain? Maybe God heard her cries for forgiveness and this was His gift to her. That in her final moments she would feel no pain.

Whatever the reason behind it, her brain decided to spare her body the agony leading to her last breath.

***

He stared down at her lifeless body. He knew just the place to leave her. Before moving her, he recited, "Dominus vobiscum." He ran his thumb over her forehead, chin, and chest in the sign of the cross to give her absolution.

As he stepped into the sultry Louisiana night a fine, steamy mist shrouded the ancient oak trees that surround the property. A heavy breeze riffled through the clumps of Spanish moss dripping from the gnarled branches of the oak trees. A heavy dew had fallen. The ground shimmered in the glow of the moonlight.

Sweat ran down his body as he loaded the victim's lifeless body in the back of the van. She was dead weight. In the distance, he could hear the tinkling of the glass bottles someone long ago attached to one of the ancient trees. He had not removed them. They were common around these parts, especially if someone was superstitious. People called them spirit bottles. Rumor had it that those who practiced in voodoo also believed in the spirit bottles. He sometimes wondered if they had any credence. When the wind blew, the noise was supposed to help keep the evil spirits away. He found it strange how at the exact moment of her death a wind blew thru the trees causing the glass to sing their tune. It was as if the wind was chasing her soul from this property.

He headed out to display this sinner's body.

It was devoid of life this early in the morning. He scanned the street one more time before transporting the body from the van to the front steps of the church.

* * *

The sun was climbing over the horizon. A jogger was out for her morning run, enjoying the solitude. She picked up speed as she rounded the corner. As she neared the church steps, she screamed. She was frozen in fear, unable to look away from the body. She fell to her knees and wrapped her arms around herself. Unable to move, she continued to scream praying someone heard her.

* * *

Picou heard his cell phone ring. It was Sheriff Riley, "Picou."

"We have a body on the front steps of St. Anthony's Catholic Church."

"Crap. When was it discovered?"

Sheriff Riley informed him, "Early this morning, right before sunrise."

"I'll call Melancon. We'll head out there now."

Picou called Melancon, "We have another body. It's at St. Anthony's Catholic Church. Do you want me to pick you up?"

"Yeah. I'll be waiting outside."

* * *

Jo was thankful that at least it wasn't raining or in the middle of the night. She was getting ready to head to the office when Picou called. She grabbed a cup of coffee and poured Chad one just in case. As she walked out the door, he pulled up. She opened the car door and handed him his coffee, "Didn't know if you needed a jolt."

Picou let out a laugh, "I never turn down coffee. I have a feeling we will need all the caffeine we can get today."

As they headed to the crime scene Melancon asked, "Do we know if this was the same killer?"

"I know that a body was found on the steps of the church, but given the religious tones I have a feeling it's our guy."

Melancon shook her head, "Me too." Melancon couldn't stop the thoughts tumbling inside of her head. She and Picou had to stop this guy before he killed again, but also before Sheriff Riley caved in to the mayor's request and brought in outside help. She wanted to be the one to nail this bastard to the wall.

By the time they made it to the crime scene a crowd of onlookers had already gathered. The medical examiner was there looking down at the body. The woman on display was naked and marred with bruises and gouges from a knife. Her long black hair cascaded down her body like a muddy stream.

Pam Benoit's face was paler than a ghost. Her killer took pride in the way he displayed the body, intent on shocking whoever found her. The gaping knife wounds were evident along the body. There were some wounds so deep that bone showed through. The corpse seemed to stare back at her with cold dead eyes. She was a bloody mess. Pam had been pretty in life, but in death, her face was what nightmares were made of. The torturous way she died was apparent on her face. Her mouth was open in a scream that never had a chance to be heard. Trails of blood and mascara streaked her face. Melancon could smell the stench of death hanging in the air. *Oh the joys of being a homicide detective.*

It was already hot and humid, and it wasn't even eight o'clock in the morning. The sun was bright against the clear blue sky.

Picou asked, "What do we have doc?"

"Certainly appears to be your killer. Your boy thinks he is ridding the world of sinners. He left another note on the body. Her death was more violent than the previous victims."

He handed the note to Picou, "Pam Benoit must repent for sloth."

It unnerved Melancon the way Dr. Harrison was seemingly unmoved by the gory scene before him. She knew deep down he cared, but he spoke in a monotone voice, whereas when she spoke her emotions were clearly noted.

Picou looked over the body and let out a shudder, "Do you have time of death?"

"I'll know more when I get her back to the morgue and perform the autopsy, but more than likely a few hours ago."

Looking around, he saw no blood so this must be another dumpsite. What a sacrilege to the Church. He heard Melancon whisper in his ear, "Heads up Mayor Daigle and Sheriff Riley are walking this way."

Picou let out a groan. He wasn't in the mood to deal with Mayor Daigle right now.

Mayor Daigle greeted the detectives, "Good morning Detectives. What have we found out so far?"

Picou looked over at Sheriff Riley before updating the men, "Well, we do know this is just another dump site. He left us another message stating that she had to repent for her sin. A good portion of the body was mutilated. We need to find out the last time anyone saw Pam and the coroner is working on a time of death. Crime scene techs are busy working, but I don't look for them to find much useable trace evidence. They did find some fibers on the body, and will get that report to us as soon as possible. Dr. Harrison will run a toxicology report to see if she was drugged the same as the others, but with the note left behind I am certain this was our killer. No defensive wounds on the body once again, so she may have known her killer."

Mayor Daigle asked, "Anything I can give the press."

Picou shook his head, "I don't have anything to give you right now. I hope we will know more after the autopsy. I will let you know as soon as the toxicology and forensics reports come in.

Melancon walked over to Robicheaux, "Did you catch the call this morning?"

He nodded his head, "The call came in a little before six o'clock this morning. A man heard the woman screaming for her life and called the cops while he ran out to see what happened. She was out jogging this morning when she saw the body on the church stairs. She is still shaken up. I called Sheriff Riley and forensics as soon as I saw what was going on."

As Picou watched the ME's office carry the body off, he told Melancon, "I think our killer is an exhibitionist. He wants these bodies found and his message known. Why else would he leave the notes?"

Melancon looked around at the gathering crowd and noticed news vans falling in behind the police cars, "Damn, it looks as if the press has made it."

Picou let out a deep groan. That was the last thing he wanted to deal with right now.

Melancon still couldn't believe that they had another victim. The killer left the body in the heart of the city, at the biggest Catholic Church in town. Their killer wasn't being subtle with his killings. The staging of the bodies was designed to capture attention. Looking around, she tried to see which routes he could have traveled to get here. Unfortunately, there were too many different ways to get in and out.

The killer had to be someone local. According to Pam Benoit's housekeeper when she left to go grocery shopping her employer was sitting on the chaise lounge watching TV. Mr. Benoit had hired a painter and when she left, he was in the back painting. The housekeeper said when she returned from shopping she found the painter gone and

Mrs. Benoit nowhere around. The housekeeper wasn't too worried, figuring she had probably gone shopping. By the time Mr. Benoit arrived home, Pam still had not returned.

There was something evil lurking in Bear Corner. The fact that it walked around on two feet all the while passing itself off as human was even more unsettling.

Picou let out a loud sigh, "This is four murders in less than eight weeks, and we are still no closer to catching this bastard."

***

Picou couldn't believe that they had another body so soon after the last one. Mia had been so understanding, once this case was over, he would have to take her somewhere romantic. They had been talking about Mexico or maybe Hawaii. They both wanted to go some place where the sunsets were breathtaking; there was plenty of sun and sand, pina coladas, and palm trees. They wanted to stroll down the beach hand in hand and watch the sun go down.

Melancon watched a media satellite van move in closer. No doubt, the ghouls were hoping to get a picture of the crime scene, or better yet a picture of the body as it was being removed. The media seemed to be getting bolder and bolder.

Chapter 36

Melancon dropped her head forward and rubbed her temples to help ward off the headache that had been lurking behind her eyes all day. Sheriff Riley had instructed them to go home and get a good night's rest, but she wanted to tie up a few loose ends before she stopped for the day. She was dead on her feet and had to stifle a yawn.

The case files on the murders were spread out on the conference room table along with the crime scene photos, evidence logs, and reports. Various officers that helped work the case had written their own summarized reports so they could compare notes to make sure nothing had been overlooked. They were not taking any chances with missing anything. It had taken hours this morning to process the crime scene.   They collected, tagged, and bagged a lot of evidence. It was still being processed.

Before leaving for the night, she checked her email to see if any reports had come in yet. Noticing that there was nothing urgent she headed home. She considered bringing the case files home to review one more time but maybe if she could get a good night's rest a fresh pair of eyes would be better.

Every time she closed her eyes, Pam Benoit's body was there waiting for her to recall every vivid detail of her murder. Not wanting to be alone she called Bill to see if he wanted to come over and discuss the case. She could give him details he may need for his story.

Bill answered on the second ring, "Hey Bill it's Jo. I was calling to see if you wanted to stop over and talk about the case."

"I was actually thinking of calling you. Have you eaten?"

"Not unless you consider something from the vending machine food."

"Why don't I pick us up some Chinese takeout?"

"Sounds like a deal to me. Do you want me to pick up some wine or beer?"

Bill told her, "No need to go through all that trouble. I still have an article I need to write."

Jo saw the drive thru daiquiri shop still open and picked them up one of their delicious concoctions. It was just what she needed after today.

After getting their drinks, she headed home. No matter how hard she tried, she couldn't stop thinking about the case. They had been investigating these murders for four months with nothing to show for it. She went over her checklist one more time. So far, the possible suspects and leads they had looked into had been a waste of time. Her mind kept replaying the crime scene this morning, seeing a husband that was now without his wife. The thought was sobering.

Looking out into the night, she knew that somewhere out there a killer was plotting his next murder. She was worried that he would not stop after the seventh deadly sin. She felt it deep in her gut that their killer was escalating. He was becoming viciously creative with the killings.

They were more than likely looking for someone who lived in the area, but she didn't see the killer as a longtime resident. They needed to look into someone who'd recently moved here or who grew up here and moved back into town. That wouldn't shorten their list though. With there being no college here, anyone who wanted to further their education had to move away for a while. She just wished there was a way to shorten their list of potential suspects.

By the time Melancon made it home, she was tired and ready to crawl under the covers. She needed a long hot shower to wash the grime of the day off of her. She smelled the stench of death embedded into her.

She pulled up at the same time as Bill did. So much for the shower, but just the sight of him sent her heart racing. He was just the distraction that she needed right now. She wondered if tonight would lead to something more. Just the thought of his lips on hers sent a shiver of desire through her. Sex may be just what she needed to take her mind off today's events, but she was getting too far ahead of herself. He was probably only interested in talking about the case.

They both got out of their cars at the same time. She held up the drinks, "I know you said that you didn't need a drink, but I couldn't resist picking up a couple of frozen concoctions from the drive thru daiquiri shop."

Bill let out a laugh, "That will go well with the Chinese food. I didn't know what you liked so I ordered a Pu Pu platter, shrimp lo mein, crispy duck and a few other dishes."

Jo breathed in the tantalizing aroma of the food and prayed he did not just hear her stomach let out a growl. "Let's get the food and drinks inside and make ourselves comfortable."

"I'm right behind you."

Jo turned on the lights as they made their way into the living room. Since she was working so much the house had stayed clean. "I've been considering moving into the sheriff's office for the duration of this case. I am rarely home right now."

Bill looked at her thoughtfully, "But if you did that I wouldn't get to stop by and have supper with you."

Jo let out a soft laugh, "Well, we can't have that now can we? I enjoy talking with you. It has been a long time since I enjoyed someone's company as much as I do yours. You are so easy to talk to, which is probably why you make such a good reporter."

"I have been told I am a natural when it comes to getting people to open up. Although, I'm not sure how I put people at ease."

Jo took a sip of her daiquiri and allowed the frozen drink to make its way down her throat, "It must have something to do with your magnetic personality."

Bill took a bite of the crispy duck, "Mm, here you have to try this. It is really good." He picked up another piece with his chopsticks and placed it in her mouth. It was a sensual move on his part and Jo wondered where the night would lead.

She took the crispy duck in her mouth and agreed, "I may have found something new to order." She picked up the coconut shrimp and placed a few on her plate. "This stuff is tasty too."

Bill looked at her plate, "Hmm, I've never tried that. I'm glad I listened to the lady taking my order." Bill leaned in and plucked a shrimp from her plate. He savored the shrimp, "You're right. This is very good. I thought it may be too sweet."

Jo shook her head, "No, it is really good. I also love their salt and pepper shrimp. The chicken is good there too."

Bill chuckled, "You sound like me. Do you cook at all?"

Jo shrugged her shoulders, "Sometimes, but I don't enjoy cooking for one person. The only problem with eating out is that I have to make sure I work off the food."

Bill looked her over, "Whatever you are doing it works. You look great."

Jo felt herself blush, unsure what to say about the compliment, "Thanks." Changing the subject, she asked, "Do you have any questions about the case."

"Actually, I gathered most of my information just by hanging out today. I am almost finished with my article. I wanted to make sure you didn't need to add anything."

Jo was surprised, "So then you know that Pam Benoit was murdered."

"Yeah, I heard the housekeeper talking about it. She was a wealth of information today."

Damn, they should have stressed to her beforehand not to talk to the press. "So what did she have to say?"

"She talked about how Pam never lifted a finger around the house and that her husband catered to her, as if she was a goddess. She also said that the husband had hired a painter to come in and paint a room in the house, but he left before the housekeeper got home."

Jo nodded her head. That had been a total dead end. The painter confirmed that he was supposed to paint the room today but had been delayed and when he arrived at the house, no one was there. He had called Mr. Benoit to inform him, but he failed to inform his wife. So now they had to find out who knew a painter was supposed to be there and why the ruse. Whoever did this was clever. They slashed all four tires on the painter's van, knowing it would take a while to have four tires fixed. He used that time to make his move. Unfortunately, the housekeeper did not get a good look at the man. She just had a general description. The "painter" that showed up at the Benoit's house kept his ball cap down low on his face and wore gloves to cover his hands. Mr. Benoit was still unsure as to who may have known a painter was coming to his house. He believed he made the arrangements at his office, but couldn't guarantee it.

Their only other lead was the painter with the slashed tires and that came up empty handed as well. The painter arrived home the night before right after nine o'clock and did not discover the slashed tires until the next morning. When the officers questioned the neighbors, no one had heard or seen anything suspicious. They just couldn't catch a break.

Bill looked at his watch, "I'm sorry. I didn't realize how late it was. I know you are tired and I need to get the article finished. Have you received any word on what happened with the painter?"

 "No. Unfortunately, we don't know who slashed his tires or even if it was our killer. Even though we have no proof, we believe our guy did this. It can't be a coincidence that his tires were slashed right before a job at the Benoit place and another individual mysteriously showed up and took his place."

Bill asked, "I guess the question is who knew that the Benoits hired a painter."

"We are trying to find out, but Mr. Benoit can't recall everyone he had told. It wasn't something he was trying to keep hidden."

Bill pulled her close and kissed her tenderly, "I wish I didn't have to rush off. Another night?"

Jo looked into his sexy eyes, "You know where I live. You may want to call first to see where I am."

"If not I know where to find you."

Jo agreed, "Yeah, I guess you do. Good night, Bill. Thanks again for supper."

"Good night Jo."

Jo watched as Bill left. She was beginning to wonder if something was wrong with her, or had she read his vibes wrong? She thought he was just as interested in her as she was in him. Maybe he was old fashioned and wanted to take his time. The other possibility, the problem that Jo ran into with all her dates, was that he didn't go for women who carried guns for a living. Men generally preferred to be the ones who rushed in to save the day. However, that was not who she was. She just did not understand. Bill's body language said that he was very interested in her, but then he walked away from her with the gentlest of kisses.

After she locked the door, she headed to the bathroom for a shower. She stepped into the shower and let the hot water pulse onto her tired body. She finished showering and towel dried her hair. As soon as she turned on her TV, she caught the latest news. *Damn!* The top story was the latest murder. She turned up the TV to hear what the reporter had to say.

"Tonight's top story is about the string of murders in Bear Corner, Louisiana. Bear Corner is recovering from Carl Ledet's murdering spree of prostitutes and now they have yet another killer on the prowl. Just this morning a passerby discovered the body of Pam Benoit on the front steps of St. Anthony's Catholic Church. Mrs. Benoit was the fifth victim murdered by this monster.

"This savage murdering spree began four months ago when the body of Victoria Russo was found in a local park. Three weeks later the body of Eric Devareaux was discovered floating in his pool. Two weeks later the body of Attorney Graham Easterly was found at the front door of his mistress, Shelia Graves, house. Food critic Brian LeBlanc's body was the next found with eerie similarities to the other deaths. It is believed that the Bear Corner Sheriff's Department is hunting down a serial killer that loves to taunt them with notes."

The next thing Melancon saw flash across the screen was a shot of all five crime scenes along with the victims' pictures. She was fuming right now. Who in the hell at the precinct leaked the press information? They had mentioned the killer leaving notes behind. She never told Bill about the notes. Did they know what the notes said? However, if they did, they would have given the serial killer a name by now.

The reporter went on to say, "Does this killer live among the fine upstanding citizens of Bear Corner, Louisiana? So far, the Sheriff's Department has no viable suspects. Sources say the list is long of those who hated both Eric Devareaux and Attorney Graham Easterly. Questions remain unanswered as to what connects the three remaining victims. What are the police doing to protect the citizens of Bear Corner from this serial killer?"

Just great! Melancon thought to herself. This was enough to send the public into a panic. The phones would be ringing off the hook soon with concerned citizens.

The reporter ended her news clip with these parting words, "The citizens of Bear Corner need to keep their doors and windows locked. Be aware of your surroundings at all times and if you see or hear anything suspicious call 911. The people of Bear Corner must be proactive right now. I can only imagine how they feel with another serial killer on the prowl."

Fuck! Melancon felt her blood pressure rising. Bill never asked her about the notes. She wondered if he knew. She knew Mayor Daigle was watching this news broadcast and compiling a list of things to chew their asses about in the morning, if he waited that long. Sheriff Riley was probably hearing about it at this moment. Nobody wanted the big boys brought in and she suspected that Mayor Daigle would push for it now. No one cared that they were working around the clock to find this killer and stop him before he struck again.

Chapter 37

Chad laid in bed, watching Mia sleep. She still wasn't sleeping well at night. He could hear her whimpering. He wished he could take away the pain from her experience with Carl Ledet. At least that monster was dead, but now he was searching for another. Another hideous creature that believed he was ridding the world of sinners.

No matter how hard Chad tried, he couldn't get this case out of his head. Every time he closed his eyes, he saw the crime scenes and the horrific tortures these victims had to endure. How did the killer know about the victims' sins? Not all were Catholic so it was not something a priest would have known. No one saw the same therapist or were in a support group of any kind. He had not found a common denominator between the victims yet. It was there. They just had to find it.

As he got out of bed, he rolled his neck in an attempt to ease the tension in his shoulders. He walked quietly through the house to the office that he and Mia now shared. He picked up his binder that he had nicknamed his "murder book" and reviewed the cases one more time. They would find this guy; he just hoped it was before someone else was murdered.

He heard a noise from the doorway. Mia was standing there watching him. With her hair mussed and her sleepy, bedroom eyes, there was no denying she was sexy. All his worries seemed to melt away when he saw her.

She joined Chad in their office and took him by his hands, and dragged him back to the bedroom. His hands found their way inside of Mia's silk robe and rested on the swell of her breasts before cupping their full weight. His thumbs brushed over her nipples. He pulled her closer to him, bringing his lips to the curve of her neck.

"You are so beautiful," he whispered in her ear.

He turned her around and took her mouth in his. He held her head captive as he devoured her mouth. She moaned and tilted her head back. Her body shivered in pleasure as he bit gently on the curve of her neck and shoulder.

***

She gasped in pleasure as one of his fingers traced her womanhood. She had never felt so cherished, so worshipped as when she was with Chad. She slid her hands into his hair and brought him closer to her. The heat of his mouth was like an inferno on her body.

His tongue traveled down her body, driving her crazy. Desire twisted through her. There was no end to what he could do with that tongue of his.

He whispered in her ear, "Touch me. You have no idea what your touch does to me."

Mia caressed him. As her hands wandered down, she felt him twitch under her fingers. She pushed him onto his back, wanting to give him the same pleasure he had given her. She traced the strong muscles of his arms and chest with her fingers. His skin rippled under her touch.

He pulled her up until she was on his lap, her womanhood pressing into his erection. He took her mouth into his and kissed her with extreme passion. Their tongues dueled with each other. They found their release at the same time. Neither could move afterwards, both were spent.

Chapter 38

Sheriff Riley called Detectives Melancon and Picou into his office. Melancon could see him fuming from here. She told Picou, "This isn't going to be a pleasant conversation."

Picou ruefully shook his head, "Mais non. I still can't figure out how in the hell the press found out about the notes. I asked the officers at the crime scene and all swore they didn't breathe a word."

Melancon had been thinking about it too, "Bill Collins was awfully quiet last night when I was talking to him. He didn't have too many questions about the recent murder. I am beginning to wonder if the killer is making contact with the press and they are not informing us."

"Mon Dieu, I hope that is not the case."

Melancon continued, "Mais, if that is the case they would have given the killer a name. I do not think they know what the notes say, just that there was one on the body."

As soon as they entered Sheriff Riley's office, they felt the tension in the air. "I want to know how in the hell the media got wind of the notes."

Picou looked at him, "We are still trying to figure that out. I chewed some ass this morning and got no answers."

Sheriff Riley slammed a fist down on his desk, "This whole damn case is going to blow up in our face." He looked over at Melancon, "I thought you were only giving the media what we wanted them to know!"

Melancon felt her anger rising, "Mais, I didn't have to tell Bill Collins any information last night. Somehow, he had most of the facts before I talked to him. He had already started writing his article."

Sheriff Riley let out a long breath, "When I find out who leaked this note business I will make…" He trailed off before letting his temper get the best of him.

It wasn't often that he came close to losing his Cajun temper, but when he did, he felt for those in his path. He may be stuck behind a desk now, but he was still a damn good cop. He had to keep reminding himself that a good cop didn't lose control. He shouldn't have gone off on the two detectives. They were fine cops. They wouldn't be where they were if they were anything less than the best.

Melancon told Sheriff Riley, "We may have to look into the fact that the killer is talking directly to the press."

"Mon Dieu. Do you think that is how the information on the note got released?"

Picou answered, "We aren't sure yet sir. If the killer had let them know about the note, he would have told them what it said."

Melancon agreed, "That is what has me stumped. Somehow they know and I am determined to find out how they caught wind of the note."

Sheriff Riley asked, "About the notes, have we been able to get any trace off of them?"

Picou shook his head, "The notes are a dead end. The paper is available at any store."

"Damn! So, we still have nothing that brings us any closer to catching this guy."

Melancon answered, "No, sir."

This case was a jigsaw puzzle and they needed to turn each of the pieces until everything fell into place. "Go back and talk to the families. Make sure we didn't miss anything in the timeline of these victims. Somehow they all came into contact with this killer."

Sheriff Riley scanned the paper one more time. He was grateful they hadn't given their killer a name. "I don't like that he is getting all of this media coverage. This may be fueling whatever is driving him."

Melancon agreed, "Yeah, but unfortunately we can't stop them from writing about him."

Melancon and Picou headed back to their desks to continue searching for a connection between the victims and the killer. They also needed to see if they were missing any gaps in the timelines. Maybe they were overlooking a tiny detail.

She picked up her coffee to take a swallow, needing the caffeine rush. She wrinkled her nose as the cold coffee hit her throat and pushed it aside.

After reviewing the timelines, she pushed them aside. She wished she knew more about the victims, but even though this was a small town, they didn't run in the same circles. If she had more details about their lives, it would be easier to point out any missing pieces.

Her grandmother's warning about being careful what you wish for ran through her mind. Right now, she would be glad to get what she wished for.

Her growling stomach reminded her that it had been a while since she had eaten. As much as she wanted to find out who the leak was in the office, she needed to grab a quick bite and worry about finding this killer. That was her top priority right now.

Chapter 39

Mia walked into the dining room of the bakery to check on things when she saw Mildred and LouAnn walking in. Mia let out a groan, knowing what these two women wanted to talk about.

"Mon Dieu, did you hear there was another murder."

Mia nodded her head, "Mais oui. That is all that is on everyone's lips this morning."

LouAnn waved her hands up in the air, "I had hoped that the killer accidentally chose the wrong person when he killed Brian LeBlanc but I can't think of anyone that Pam Benoit would have made mad. That woman barely lifted a finger to do anything."

LouAnn pulled them in closer, "I want to know what these people did to this person to make him mad enough to kill them. Mon Dieu, I don't think we have ever had this many murders in this town. Of course, that doesn't include Carl Ledet, but he mainly killed prostitutes from N'Awlins."

Mildred chimed in, "Mais oui, dere's been more murders here in Bear Corner in da past few months dan dere's been in my lifetime. It's out of control I tell you."

LouAnn shook her head, "Mais everyone I know is scared to death that this killer isn't finished yet."

Mia looked at the ladies, "I sure hope he is finished, but I fear Mildred is right."

Chapter 40

Chad stared at the ceiling. It was two o'clock in the morning and sleep still eluded him. He doubted he would fall asleep. The images of the murdered victims ran through his mind like a bad horror film.

Pushing back the covers, being careful not wake Mia, he slipped on a pair of boxers and walked into the kitchen. He turned on the light above the sink, started a pot of coffee, and set up his laptop on the table.

Once the coffee was done, he reached into the cabinet to get a coffee cup. Chad caught his reflection in the kitchen window and nearly scared himself. The harsh light almost made him look dangerous. It was from the lack of sleep and worry over another murder.

He winced at the bitter taste of the strong coffee. After adding sugar and cream, he settled down to review the files once more. He had worked enough of these cases to know his mind would not slow down until they caught this killer. Until then he would be living on coffee and lack of sleep.

They were no closer to catching this person than when they discovered the body of Victoria Russo, the first victim. He had hoped by now they would have come across something that remotely resembled a lead with all the legwork they had put into the case but so far, everything had been a dead end.

Every day that passed with no suspects or leads meant another step closer to the trail growing cold.

Looking out the window at the moonless night he feared this was the calm before the storm. It wouldn't be long before the need to kill consumed the murderer once again.

Chapter 41

Sheriff Riley paced in his office as he contemplated this case. The media presence was growing in this town. You couldn't step outside of the Sheriff's Office without running into a news van, camera crew or a reporter trying to ask a question.

Then you had the curiosity seekers hanging out downtown. They milled about hoping to catch a rumor of what was going on with the investigation. The vendors in front of the courthouse were extremely busy with all the people around. Andre, Sheriff Riley's favorite, loved all the business. He couldn't keep up with the boudin and Andouille corn dog sales. He was also selling alligator on a stick and bowls of Pierre's gumbo. The enticing aromas made your mouth water as soon as you stepped outside.

They had absolutely no leads and their list of suspects was staggering. They had slowly been exonerating most on that list. Just about everyone who wanted Devareaux and Easterly dead had solid alibis.

He walked over to the conference room to see if they had any updates. Detective Melancon was looking over the board when he walked in the room, "Anything new to tell me."

She ruefully shook her head, "No sir. I sure wish I did. I am trying to track their movements. There has to be one place that they all went, but I am not having any luck. With this being a small town you would think their paths would have crossed a few times, but locating that point is turning out to be an impossible task. Benoit and Russo did not share the same tastes as Devareaux and Easterly. The two men had extravagant tastes, more than what the two women could afford, even with their wealth. LeBlanc was out there all by himself as well."

Sheriff Riley perused the crime scene photos, "What on earth could set off another human being to do something so cruel to another person?"

Melancon shook her head, "I just don't know sir. I think the gaps in between the killings are when he stalks his victims to make sure that they are sinners and to find the perfect time to kill them."

Sheriff Riley agreed, "You are probably correct in your assumption. If he is this determined to kill those committing a deadly sin, he would want confirmation first. Devareaux and Easterly were easy choices, but everyone was surprised by Russo, LeBlanc, and Benoit."

"Exactly, there is a reason the victims were not strangers to him. Somehow, he got to know them, knew their lives and their routines. Something they did set him off."

Melancon continued with her observations, "There is a chance that the stalking is part of his ritual."

Sheriff Riley asked, "You don't think he already had his seven picked out before he started killing do you?"

Melancon contemplated the question, "No, I don't think he has his list of people just yet. If that were the case, then the time in between killings would be shorter. Something tells me that he has to confirm the person is a sinner before he kills them. I have a feeling he has been watching everyone in this town, biding his time before having his plan come to fruition. He needed to make sure the people here trusted him before he started killing. If a stranger were to come in and start lurking about at night people would be wary, especially after Carl Ledet."

Sheriff Riley let out a sigh, "What bothers me is that even though the killings seem to have a frenzied look to them, I think he is cool and calm while executing these murders."

Chapter 42

Jo heard from Bill several days later, "I am calling to see how the investigation is going."

She replied, "I wish I could tell you I have some updates, but so far we have nothing concrete to give anyone. This killer doesn't leave behind enough evidence to go on."

"What about the notes?"

"I'm not sure what the media believes they have on the notes, but that is not something we can divulge right now."

Bill asked, "So I guess that I have to wait until you can tell me something more solid."

"Unfortunately, yes."

"Well then, since we don't have to talk about the case, how would you like to go get something to eat? I would like to take you to a real sit down restaurant and talk."

Jo felt the anticipation building up inside of her, "I would love that. When would you like to meet?"

"Are you busy tonight? I have finished my article for tomorrow and am free."

"Let me get things wrapped up here and I can make myself free for a little while. What time would you like to meet and where?"

Bill asked, "How about Marcel's in an hour?"

"I can manage that."

"Do you want me to pick you up?"

Jo looked at her watch one more time, "No, I am downtown and can just meet you there. I hope you don't mind that I am not too dressed up."

Jo was so glad she'd worn one of her nicer pant suits today. She just needed to touch up her makeup. She couldn't believe that Bill Collins asked her out for supper. She shouldn't read too much into the invitation, but her heart raced in anticipation of seeing him for a reason other than to talk about the case.

It took Jo a short time to finish everything she had to do before leaving for the day. Once done, she bolted before something came up that required her to stay at the office longer.

She ran into the bathroom to check her face and make sure her clothes still looked decent. The black pants were a lightweight material that held up well during the course of the day and the red silk blouse helped show off the twinkle in her eyes.

By the time she arrived at the restaurant Bill was waiting outside for her. "I hope I didn't keep you waiting too long."

He smiled, "Nope, I just got here myself."

When they stepped inside the hostess seated them right away. Jo was quite surprised. Usually this restaurant was crowded. She asked, "Aren't y'all usually packed at this time of the night."

The hostess shook her head, "Normally, we have a line out the door, but with the killer on the prowl people don't want to venture out at night." Jo couldn't help but take the empty restaurant personally. They had to catch this guy. She hated that people didn't feel safe in their hometown. Until the killer was behind bars, people would stay at home with their doors bolted.

There were only a few patrons in the restaurant. With the soft music playing in the background it was as if they had the back corner to themselves. From where they were seated, you wouldn't even know that there were other customers.

While they ate their supper, they talked about their childhoods and shied away from the investigation. Jo was grateful he didn't talk about the case. She had had enough of it for one day.

When the waiter stopped to clear their plates and asked if they wanted dessert, Jo perused the menu, not ready for the night to end, "Hmmm, the tuxedo cake sounds heavenly. May I please have that with a cup of coffee?"

The waiter asked Bill, "And you, sir?"

Bill looked up from the menu, "I would like the bread pudding with amaretto sauce and a cup of coffee."

The waiter finished clearing the table, "I will be right back with your desserts."

Jo looked over at Bill, "Thank you very much for this lovely evening. Ever since this case, or maybe a little before, I haven't had much of a social life."

"I find you fascinating and wanted to talk to you about something other than the case."

"It is nice to have a conversation about something other than murder and mayhem. Cases like this cut into one's personal life."

Bill shook his head, "Isn't it amazing what we give up for our careers?"

"It is. I tend to run men off when they hear that I am a homicide detective."

Bill replied, "That's ludicrous. You are a gorgeous woman. I assumed you had men beating your door down."

She let out a faint laugh, "No such luck there. I think the gun turns them away."

Bill let out a soft chuckle, "Yeah, I guess I never thought about that. It may be hard for some men to overcome. But I have a feeling once someone gets to know you, they would find you just as intriguing as I do."

They looked up as the waiter brought their desserts and coffee. The chocolate tuxedo cake looked sinful. Jo took a forkful of the dessert and moaned in pleasure. "Oh my goodness! This is completely wicked. I'm going to have to run an extra mile in the morning for sure."

Bill took a bite of his bread pudding and smiled, "I must say their desserts have gotten a lot better since they started ordering from Mia."

"I don't know how Chad stays so fit. If I were around Mia's food all day, I would weigh a ton. Everything she makes is delicious."

Bill agreed, "She is sitting on a gold mine. What I love is that she offers a variety. When you walk into her shop in the morning, you never know what she will have to offer. The only thing that stays the same is the quality of the food, the beignets, and café au lait."

"I sometimes feel sorry for poor Chad. I think she works just as hard as he does. He mentioned the other day that Mia planned to hire more help."

"She would be a fool not to. She will run herself ragged if she doesn't."

Jo replied, "That is what Chad and her parents tell her. She doesn't have to worry about the extra overhead either. I have no doubt she will be able to absorb the extra costs."

"Will she do it or is she one of those who has to have complete control?"

"Not Mia. I have never met a more unselfish person than her. She is concerned about not being able to offer another person forty hours a week. I reminded her that there are plenty of stay at home moms that would love a part time job while their child is in school. I look for her to place an ad any day now."

***

Bill was glad Jo brought up Mia. He often wondered what kind of person she was since Carl Ledet killed prostitutes and sinners. He had often wondered if that was what had brought Mia into the killer's sights. She seemed genuinely nice, but he knew that often looks could be deceiving.

Chapter 43
Lust

Grace Aucoin let herself into the hotel room and got ready for her lover. Her time was limited today and she did not want to waste a second of it. She had been indulging in these erotic affairs for quite some time. Whenever her schedule allowed she had hot, steamy sex with no strings attached. Why couldn't women enjoy sex just as much as a man?

She was naked except for the black fishnet stockings on her legs. While waiting for him to arrive, she practiced several different poses, trying to figure out which way she wanted to be when he walked into the room.

Desire coursed through her body as she waited in anticipation for her lover to get here. She hoped he arrived soon.

***

He watched as she placed the key under the doormat for her lover. He gave her a few minutes to prepare herself before he moved in. He left a message for the man at work, telling him something came up and they had to postpone their tryst. The secretary thought nothing of taking the message for her boss.

He felt nothing but hatred for this woman who lusted after a man other than her husband. She was expecting her lover to come to this dingy hotel room and instead she would find him.

His emotions were a blur as he plunged the knife into her, faster and harder. He felt his control slipping. It would be better if he didn't have emotions.

His eyes were fierce, almost savage, and filled with pure hatred. He narrowed them as he looked down at her. His hard face was bleak and bitter. Anger permeated every inch of his expression.

***

The seething intensity of his fury stunned her.

He asked her, "Are you ready to atone for your sins harlot?"

She desperately tried to make sense of what he was saying. Panic surged through her body. An animal instinct and elemental will to survive took over. She pulled against the restraints as hard as she could. Her attempts were in vain, they were too tight. Fear ran in rivulets down her back. She was in the presence of true evil. It was thick and heavy in the air, as thick as the fog that hung over the bayou in the early morning hours.

She watched as he raised the knife again. She tried to prepare herself for what was about to happen, this was how he would kill her. Time seemed to stop. The knife plunged into her abdomen once more. The pain was excruciating. The gag in her mouth muffled her screams.

Never in her life had she ever endured the amount of pain she was experiencing right now. She prayed that the hurt would be too much and she drifted off into unconsciousness, sparing her the agony she was suffering right now.

***

He had no pity for her; she was a sinner. He had no second thoughts about killing her. She brought this upon herself by tempting men other than her husband. Her body shuddered as her life slipped away. She never repented for her sins. He wondered if God would forgive her.

There was so much blood oozing from her body. Unable to stop himself, he continued to plunge the knife deeper into her body. Death had released her from the pain he was inflicting.

Looking down at her dead body there was something strangely intimate about her cold and brutal death. Black pools of blood formed on the bed. Her naked body was ravaged by the stab wounds.

No one heard her cries for mercy as he savagely attacked her. Soon the town would know of her sin, how she lusted after another man.

Grace Aucoin was a desirable woman. If she had not strayed from her husband, she would still be alive.

As he looked over the dead sinner one last time, he recited as God instructed, "Dominus vobiscum." His blood sang at the thought of a soul being set free. Slowly he ran his thumb over her forehead, chin, and chest in the sign of the cross. He gave her absolution.

***

The next morning the housekeeper found the body when she entered the room. She woke up the remaining guests

with her incessant screaming. In the middle of the bed lay a
woman bound and gagged, brutally murdered and
eviscerated. Her soulless eyes stared up at nothing.

Chapter 44

When Picou arrived at the hotel, he greeted the young officer standing guard. He shook his head at the thought of another crime scene. He asked, "Has Melancon made it here yet?"

"She's inside, sir."

From the doorway, he could see technicians brushing the room for prints. This place was a nightmare with the amount of prints they would recover, and how would they know which ones belonged to their killer. The only good thing that came from the murder taking place at the hotel room was this time they had an actual crime scene to work with and from the looks of it, the killer didn't bother to clean up. Maybe, they would get lucky and find something he left behind.

The smell of death hit Picou as soon as he walked into the hotel room. The metallic odor of blood was overpowering. He doubted housekeeping would ever get rid of the smell. They had to collect the blood soaked mattress. Blood had seeped all the way through. Grotesque blood splatter patterns marked the wall and ceiling. Their killer was definitely frenzied.

Picou frowned down at the body. For a moment, he thought he would be sick as he looked at the carnage.

A police photographer was busy taking pictures of the crime scene. There were numerous blood splatter striations on the walls. "Did we get pictures of the body?"

Melancon replied, "Yeah."

Picou yanked on a pair of latex gloves. "What kind of sick freak are we dealing with?"

"Aren't they all sick and twisted?"

Dr. Harrison finally arrived and observed the body. Melancon asked, "Does it look like she was raped doc?"

"I'm not sure yet. I'll swab for semen. There is so much mutilation, multiple stab wounds, and blood splatter. He also came prepared. He tied her up and gagged her."

From the extent of the rope burns on her wrists and ankles, she did not give up easily. She was a fighter. Her eyes showed the terror she went through before she died. This fucking bastard put her through hell.

Picou instructed the crime scene techs, "Remove the ropes carefully. Make sure we bag her hands. Maybe we will get lucky and find some DNA in the rope knots."

"Yes, sir." One of the techs carefully removed the ropes.

Dr. Harrison told the detectives, "The cuts were deep. When I get her to the morgue, I will examine her in detail. Maybe this time he left evidence on the body."

Picou felt a headache starting at the base of his skull and his stomach was in knots. What kind of monster did this? Their killer was definitely a psychotic exhibitionist. He was staging the bodies and sending them a message. So far, he had claimed the victims were sinners and had to repent.

Looking over the body their killer was getting a taste for killing.

One of the crime scene techs called from the bathroom, "Detectives, it looks as if your killer cleaned up in the bathroom before he left."

Melancon asked, "So do you think her husband knew she was fooling around?"

Picou answered, "If he did then at least we will have a viable suspect but I doubt it. The manager said that she was a regular. He never saw the man, just her. Maybe she met her husband here for a little afternoon delight. Hell for all we know it could have been a game to them."

"We need to talk to the husband and see if he was the one she was meeting here. This time Picou, it is your turn to ask."

Picou laughed at her, "What's wrong? Can't take telling another spouse that their significant other was having an affair?"

"Honestly, no! I did not know we had so many cheating spouses in this town. Here I thought these people were happily married and now I find out just how wrong I am."

Picou replied, "Yeah, but the big question is who in this town knew their dirty little secrets."

Melancon watched as the crime scene techs collected evidence. It was probably a complete waste of time. So far, the results had given them a big fat goose egg. The blood had all come from the victims. How could someone mutilate another individual and not at least nick themselves? This was one lucky bastard. The cotton fibers found at the scene came from any one of a thousand sources and no trace or any other forensic evidence was found on the bodies. It was as if a ghost performed these murders.

Picou looked over the body, "Our guy likes to slash and carry."

Chad held the note that was now safely in an evidence bag, Grace Aucoin must repent for LUST."

Frustration raged through him as he observed the crime scene, trying to look at it through the killer's eyes. He looked up to the ceiling asking the Lord for help. This was going to be a long day.

Chapter 45

When Grace Aucoin's husband, Dan, opened the door, Picou could tell he was shocked to see them there. Dan greeted them, "Chad what brings you this way?"

Picou asked him, "Did you have plans to meet Grace for lunch?"

"No, she told me she had several errands to run today and she would be late. I was getting ready to call her to see where she is."

This was the part Picou hated the most, "Dan, why don't you have a seat?"

He looked at Chad, "Why? What's going on?"

He patted Dan on the shoulder, "I have something to tell you, but you should be sitting down when you hear this."

Shock registered across Dan's face, "No, you must be mistaken. Grace is just running late. She said that she had some errands to run today."

"Dan, let's go sit in the living room."

Picou watched as sorrow moved across Dan's face, "Oh God no. You're wrong. It can't be Grace." His eyes implored Chad to tell him this was a huge mistake.

He hated being the one to deliver this crushing blow, but he had no choice.

"Dan, I'm so sorry. We found Grace's body this afternoon.
She's gone."

Dan let out a heart-wrenching sob and fell to his knees.
Picou helped him off the floor and led him to a chair. He
didn't know what to say that would ease the pain and it was
only going to get worse.

"Dan, is there someone I can call for you? Someone who
can come over and sit with you."

 "No, I just want to be alone."

Picou felt like a heel, "Dan, I need to ask you a few other
questions. Does Grace have an address book or laptop that
we can look at?"

"Yeah, I think so. Why?"

"We need to know who she was meeting for lunch if it
wasn't you."

Dan looked at him with suspicion in his eyes, "Exactly how
and where was my wife killed Chad?"

"Mon ami, she was killed at a local hotel. The manager said
she has a standing lunch date on Thursdays. We need to
find out who it was with."

***

Dan felt his world come crashing down around him. He
grabbed the laptop from the bedroom, "Take it, and take
whatever the hell else you need. I can't believe the lying,
cheating bitch would do this to me. Now I know why she

wasn't ready to start a family just yet. She swore she was completely devoted to me and our marriage."

***

He cooked himself a hearty breakfast this morning consisting of eggs over easy with grits, crispy bacon, wheat toast and coffee. Grace Aucoin confirmed his suspicions last night. She fought and used foul language when he told her to beg for redemption. Her attitude fortified that her soul needed cleansing. Sitting at the kitchen table, he lifted the coffee cup to his lips when the morning's newspaper article caught his eye. Fury raged through him, no one seemed to understand the importance of his work.

The police vowed to stop him, but they couldn't, no one could. With God on his side, how could he fail? God's mission was righteous. His plan was meticulous and he was almost done releasing the sinners. Once his mother's soul was released from purgatory, his mission would be complete. If this mission failed to absolve her, he would move on to another city.

Chapter 46

Sheriff Riley called in Detectives Picou and Melancon. When Picou saw Mayor Russ Daigle also sitting in the office, he knew this wasn't a normal pow wow.

Mayor Daigle looked over at the detectives, "So detectives are we out of our element here?"

Picou rubbed his growing beard as he contemplated the best way to answer this question. He feared that Sheriff Riley had set them up, but one look at his face and Chad realized that the Sheriff had no idea the mayor was going to ask the question.

Upon further examination, Picou noticed how jittery the mayor was. He was normally calm and collected, this morning he was far from either.

Although the question aggravated Picou, he needed to answer this in a way that showed their ability to handle this case. He refused to be pulled from the case when they were getting close to solving it.

He knew that the mayor didn't like the obstacles he was currently facing. These murders were gruesome and causing uneasy feelings in the residents of Bear Corner.

Sheriff Riley stepped in, "Mayor Daigle we have the town's finest detectives working on this case. They have been compiling evidence and they want to catch this guy just as bad as you do, if not more. Trust me, if they felt they were out of their element and this case was too much for them, they would be the first to ask for assistance. Right now we don't have enough to bring the FBI in on and the state trooper's have their hands full."

Melancon spoke up, "Mayor Daigle you have nothing to worry about. We will track this killer down." She said it with as much conviction as she could muster. However, she was not sure she convinced anyone in the room.

Irritation flashed through Mayor Daigle's eyes, "So tell me Detective, just what should I tell the concerned citizens that call me at all hours of the day and night? I don't think that informing the public we have the best detectives working the case will help put their minds at ease, do you? I don't want to hear excuses. I want you to catch this sick fucker. I want the criminal element here in Bear Corner shaking in their boots. This is supposed to be a peaceful town, but ever since that damn Carl Ledet people are scared to go out at night. We don't need the worry of violent crime here."

Sheriff Riley wondered if Mayor Daigle was causing him this much of a headache because he wanted this motherfucker caught as bad as they did or if it was part of his political agenda.

Picou looked over at Sheriff Riley before he divulged too much information. When Sheriff Riley nodded, Picou handed everyone a copy of the trace evidence reports from the crime scenes. "I believe we are making headway. Our killer finally left us some evidence that we can go on. Not only did he leave the crime scene in disarray, but he also showered in the hotel room. The crime scene techs procured several strands of pubic hair with a follicle attached."

Mayor Daigle perked up, "So we may have this asshole's DNA?"

Melancon nodded her head, "Yes sir. Unfortunately, he isn't in CODIS but it gives us enough to pull suspects in for matches. We are doing background checks on the newcomers in town, just to be on the safe side. I have a hard time believing that someone who has lived here all their life is committing these murders, but we can't rule that prospect out. We need to look at people that moved into town right before the killings started as well. I have checked VICAP and so far, there have been no hits. That doesn't mean another small town hasn't had unsolved murders like ours. I sent out a request to the law enforcement agencies and I hope that we get a response. If we do, then we can compare their possible suspects to ours. Maybe we will get lucky and they have someone who moved away after the killings stopped."

Picou went on in further detail, "According to the notes left at each scene, our killer is murdering victims he believes committed one of the seven deadly sins. Victoria Russo was pride, Eric Devareaux was greed, Graham Easterly was wrath, Brian LeBlanc was gluttony, Pam Benoit was sloth, and Grace Aucion was lust. Now to find this guy before we have victim seven, envy."

Mayor Daigle absorbed everything they were telling him, "What do you suspect will happen when he reaches victim seven?"

Melancon answered, "That is another part of the problem. If he has done this in another town, then he will more than likely move on. If this is his first time, then we have to worry that he will move on to another dynamic for killing. I doubt this guy will stop. There are enough religious zealots out there that can find sin in just about anything."

"Well then let's catch this guy before he kills again."

That was easier said than done. They were getting closer to solving this puzzle. He hoped it would be before he killed again. The time in between the kills was getting shorter.

Detective Melancon let out a sigh of relief when Mayor Daigle left. She had not been sleeping well since the second murder. She took a sleeping pill last night, but it did not help. She could not get these murders out of her mind. She had never seen so much death.

Melancon looked over at Picou, "This guy is bound to get careless. I hate knowing that he is out there walking the streets of Bear Corner. I don't want to tell another spouse that their loved one is dead and I sure as hell don't want to be the one to tell them their partner was unfaithful."

Sheriff Riley looked over at Melancon, "Why don't you leave early and update Bill Collins. Maybe he can spin this in a way to make the killer believe we have some solid evidence, shake his tree so to speak."

Melancon was worried what would happen if they did rattle the guy too much though, "I'll call Mr. Collins to see if he is up to meeting this afternoon."

"Good, good. In addition, it can't hurt for the public to know that the Sheriff's Office has been working around the clock. Let them know the lab has rushed the DNA analysis on the hairs found at the scene."

"Yes, sir."

Picou asked Sheriff Riley, "Do you think the mayor will try to get the FBI involved?"

"I think we gave him enough information where he will hold off for now. Besides, the Feds won't be interested in this case. It isn't high profile enough for them."

Melancon asked, "What about letting it slip about the connection the victims share?"

Picou shook his head, "I think that is something we need to hold off on. We don't need another nutcase out there wanting to commit any copycat murders."

Sheriff Riley agreed, "We can inform them that we have found a possible connection, but we can't go into further detail. Tell Collins that we are connecting the dots."

"Yes, sir."

Chapter 47

Melancon saw the evidence clerk heading toward their desks, "Detectives we just got the DNA reports back from the Aucoin crime scene."

Melancon perked up at that comment, "Please tell me we got something."

The evidence clerk nodded his head, "We got something. Unfortunately, there was no match in CODIS, but at least it is something solid."

Picou rubbed his hands together, "Finally, we are making headway. We need to nail this guy before he takes another life."

Melancon didn't want to get her hopes up, "I want to catch this guy just as bad as you, but how do we do that when we don't have a match in CODIS."

Jo reviewed the report the evidence clerk just brought to them. Now if they only had a suspect to go with the DNA. They needed something solid to bring someone in and they just didn't have that. If it were up to Melancon, she would make everyone in town line up for a DNA analysis. She knew that was just wishful thinking.

No matter how hard she tried, she couldn't take her mind off of this case. Whenever she passed people, she wondered if they were the killer. What made it worse was the killer might be someone she knew. Could she possibly talk to this person every day and not know that he was capable of committing these heinous murders?

She tried to picture what he might look like, but it was just so hard to picture a normal person committing these crimes. Evil should look like a malicious monster and not the person living right next door to you. Nevertheless, evil was deceptive. It wouldn't be ugly until it was ready to show its true self and by then it was too late. It wanted to make itself hard to recognize because that was what evil did best, deceive.

At first evil was charming and knew the right words to say. It drew you in, made you trust it and then when you least expected it evil would show its soulless eyes. By then it was too late.

Their killer had to be physically fit to drive a large knife into the bodies and dispose of them after death. Just the thought of the pain they endured sent a shiver through her body. The person who committed these crimes had an extreme amount of rage going through his body at the time of the killings. She wondered if he felt guilty afterwards or if he was like most killers and felt no remorse.

Chapter 48

Jo called Bill to see if he wanted to meet with her and she knew the best place in town to drop a rumor. As usual, he answered on the second ring, "Bill, I have an update to give you on the case. I was wondering if you would be interested in meeting at Cherie's for a drink and I can tell you what all we have found out."

"I take it you must have something good then. Are you sure you want to meet somewhere so public."

The wheels were turning in Jo's mind, "Absolutely positive. After the day I have had, a little celebration is in order."

Now Bill's curiosity was piqued, "Does this mean you may make an arrest soon?"

"I'll discuss more when we are together."

They agreed to meet at the bar at six o'clock that evening. Jo knew by that time Cherie's would be packed. It was time to set her plan into motion.

When she arrived at Cherie's, Bill was waiting for her. This place was one of her favorite hangouts. It may not be a distinguished nightclub, but the crowd here was a bunch of good ole Cajuns who knew how to have a good time. The food was delicious and the drinks weren't watered down. Here the regulars knew each other and newcomers were always welcome.

The sound of zydeco music greeted them as soon as they entered. Pierre waved to her from the bar, "Cher, Mon

Dieu it's been a while since you have graced these walls. Mais, to what do we owe this pleasure."

Jo smiled over at her good friend, "I came to kick back and relax. We finally caught a break in the case and I want to celebrate."

Pierre came over and gave her a big bear hug, "Mon Dieu, it's about time cher."

Bill watched the interaction between the two from veiled eyes. He wondered what they had that had put such a smile on her face. They found a table near the bar and made themselves comfortable.

Their server came over and took their drink orders. Melancon told the waitress she wanted one of Pierre's frozen concoctions, "Surprise me with something yummy, and bring us each a plate of whatever he is cooking."

The waitress let out a soft laugh, "And you sir."

"I'll just have a beer."

***

Bill noticed how comfortable Jo was around here. Her face seemed to relax as soon as she entered. He had never been much for the bar scenes, but this place had a certain atmosphere about it. You could smell the food cooking in the back.

Bill swore that as soon as they sat down the music dropped several notches. No doubt wanting to catch tidbits of anything they talked about. He wondered if anyone remembered that curiosity killed the cat.

Bill asked Jo, "So does your partner know you are talking to me?"

"I may have mentioned it in passing. Why?"

Bill shrugged his shoulders, "You two seem very close is all."

"We make a good team. We seem to click on most things; we are more like brother and sister than partners. When we don't see eye to eye we bicker back and forth."

Bill agreed, "I must say from what I have observed during this investigation, you two seem to be an impressive duo."

"We both want the same thing. To stop this guy before he kills again."

"And I take it you discovered something today that brings you one step closer to that."

Jo leaned in to him, but made sure she said it loud enough for someone to hear, "We found DNA at the last crime scene. He thought he was being so careful, but he forgot to check the drain in the bathtub."

"So what makes you think the killer was the one that took a shower and not just another guy staying there?"

"We considered that, but the manager said it had been a while since the room was rented out. Actually, the last person that used the room before the murder was Grace Aucoin and her lover last week. That was their weekly ritual. Once we found out the name of her lover, we removed his hairs from the scene and it left us with the perp's."

Bill let out a whistle, "I'm impressed. That is some pretty good detective work."

Jo smiled over at him, "Sometimes our jobs aren't so different you know. No one likes to see us head towards them, not wanting to answer our questions. We both have to dig into people's lives and most of those we question want their secrets to remain hidden."

"You find our jobs similar then?"

Jo responded, "In a roundabout way they are. You can't tell me that you haven't run into any undeserved narrow-mindedness along the way."

Something dangerous flashed in his eyes for a moment, and then quickly went away. She must have touched a raw nerve there. Maybe she was cracking through his tough outer shell. He replied, "I'll admit that we get those that cringe when they see us heading their way. Cops are the worst."

Jo put her arms up in surrender, "I admit we tend to judge the press. But you have to admit you show up at the most inopportune times."

"We want to keep the public well informed."

Jo reluctantly agreed, "I realize the public needs to be kept informed, but it doesn't help us when the public breaks out in a mass panic. Especially when they are walking around armed and jumping at shadows."

Bill glanced at his watch, "If I want to get my story out on time I need to get going."

Jo followed him out. It must be later than she thought. It was pitch black outside now. When they reached her car, he took her in his arms and kissed her before opening her car door. "Good night Jo. I'll call you later."

"Good night Bill."

The kiss left her wanting so much more. She wondered if his kisses would ever lead to anything more. Maybe once this case was over he would make a move. He might be one of those that did not like to mix business with pleasure.

Chapter 49

Mia sat on the back porch with a glass of Moscato to ease the day's tension. She inhaled the smell of the bayou mingled with the damp earth and pine trees, letting it calm her.

The full moon shined brightly, hiding the stars and exposing a layer of fine white haze that hovered ghostlike over the bayou. An owl hooted from somewhere nearby and she mimicked its sound. It thrilled her when it responded back. Near the bayou, she heard a rustling and wondered if an alligator was on the prowl.

It was magnificent here. She loved coming out back and relaxing from a hard day at the bakery. After Carl Ledet abducted her, she found it very difficult to come outside, but the beauty of the area won out and her fears slowly abated. Chad helped her through that rough period. He kept telling her that she could not let Carl Ledet and what happened defile how she felt about this place.

The door opened and she heard footsteps, "I figured I would find you back here." Chad sat next to her on the swing and wrapped an arm around her shoulders, pulling her in closer.

Mia smiled up at him before reaching up and placing a kiss on his lips.

Chapter 50

Alex Hamilton saw the article from The Tribune in Bear Corner, Louisiana and it piqued his interest. He had just finished writing another book that was guaranteed to be a best seller and had been on the lookout for another venture before writing another book. This may be just what he needed.

His wife, Sheriff Jordan Hamilton, carried their beautiful one-year-old daughter to her room. He walked up behind her while she was at the crib and nuzzled her neck. He whispered in her ear as to not wake up the sleeping baby, "She looks so much like you."

Jordan smiled up at him and kissed him on the lips. She pulled him out of the room and gently shut the door. "I know that look in your eyes. What's on your mind?"

He pulled her into his arms, "Why must there be something on my mind?"

"I've been married to you over two years now. I know when you have something on your mind."

Alex asked, "How far is Bear Corner from here?"

Jordan thought about it for a moment, "I'm not sure. We can check it out for sure on MapQuest, but I believe it is almost four hours. It may even be closer to five. If I remember correctly, it is near the Mississippi/Louisiana border. Why?"

"I saw a newspaper article where they have had six murders with almost the same MO. I am thinking about riding down there in the morning to check things out."

Jordan shuddered at the thought of having to catch another serial killer. She could go the rest of her life without having to deal with that. Her heart went out to the town. "Something tells me that you have already done some research."

Alex nodded, "I may have looked it up on the internet. I found at least ten articles written by a Bill Collins with The Tribune, along with several articles written by another New Orleans newspaper and various other papers. If these articles are correct, it sounds as if they have a serial killer. What makes it worse is it comes right after the town is recovering from a previous attack by another serial killer who was dumping prostitutes in the bayous there."

Something clicked in Jordan's memory, "I heard something about that. This man was killing prostitutes from New Orleans, claiming he was cleansing their souls and then sinking their bodies into the bayou. So far they have only identified a few of the bodies."

Alex nodded his head in agreement, "That sounds like the case. A Carl Ledet from there killed a few women in the town and abducted another local woman who was saved at the last minute."

Jordan looked at him, "Do you want me to give the sheriff a call and suggest that you look at the case?"

Alex grimaced at that suggestion, "No, I don't think it would go over well if my wife called for me."

Jordan shrugged her shoulders, "I thought it might just help you get your foot in the door. It's not like you can tell him you were with the FBI."

"Actually, I'm hoping that is what helps me get my foot in the door. If they know I am no longer with the FBI, but was one of their top profilers it may be my best advantage. That way the sheriff doesn't have to worry about the feds coming in and taking over."

Jordan pulled him closer to her and kissed him, "You may be right. Just be forewarned those Cajuns down there are territorial."

Alex kissed her back, "Then that may be when I need my big, bad sheriff wife to call and talk me up."

Jordan let out a laugh. "If you need me to help you I have no problem doing it. I have faith in you though. You won me over."

"That I did."

The next morning when Alex's alarm clock went off at three o'clock he was excited to get on the road. He felt that old adrenaline rush when he was about to profile a new case. He did not regret leaving the FBI to write books and be near his true love, Jordan Sanders, but at times he missed being in the field. Whenever he felt the walls closing in on him, he perused the papers to see if there was a possible serial killer on the loose. Since he left the FBI, he had helped profile and stop four more serial killers. He hoped that

Sheriff Riley with Bear Corner Sheriff's Department realized he was there to offer help and allowed him the chance to do so. If Alex was correct in his assumptions, then this man had hit before and once he was done in Bear Corner he would move on to another unsuspecting city.

If his initial profile was correct, then this serial killer did not intend to get caught. He considered himself on a mission that had to be completed. He had a clear and set plan.

It was after seven thirty in the morning when he pulled up to the Sheriff's Office in Bear Corner. The town was larger than he expected. From what information he'd obtained online, Bear Corner was a town rich in Cajun heritage.

Alex walked into the Sheriff's Office and looked around. He had half expected to find the place to be a ghost town, instead there was a flurry of activity. He wondered, or maybe feared, that they were close to capturing the serial killer. If they did not need his help, he hoped that they at least allowed him to talk to the serial killer.

A young officer finally came up to the front desk, "I'm sorry sir. I stepped away just for a moment. If you are with the press, you may as well step back outside. Sheriff Riley will make a statement later on, I'm sure."

Alex shook his head and held out his hand, "My name is Alex Hamilton and I am a profiler. I came to offer my assistance to Sheriff Riley and the detectives."

The young officer looked at him skeptically, "I don't remember the sheriff saying anything about inviting the FBI in."

"I am no longer with the FBI. I have taken a leave of absence, but noticed a newspaper article in The Tribune about six people being brutally murdered here and thought I could lend a hand. I specialize in profiling unique killers."

The young man scratched his head, "Let me go get Sheriff Riley. I can't promise that he will talk to you though. He is awfully busy."

Alex watched as the young man left down a corridor to the right of the room. Alex felt his gut clench. He didn't want to ask Jordan to make a call for him, but if that was the only way in then he had no qualms about doing just that.

It wasn't long when Alex saw the young man return with another person, but this time it was a female. Alex felt his stomach drop, Sheriff Riley must not want to talk to him after all. "Mr. Hamilton, my name is Detective Jo Melancon. Sheriff Riley asked that I come out here to get you. We are in the middle of a pow wow."

Alex wasn't sure how to read this, but he followed her on back. "Now if I understand Officer Diaz correctly, you are no longer with the FBI, but are a profiler?"

"Yes, I helped catch the serial killer that plagued Hope, Louisiana several years back."

Detective Melancon stopped and looked at him, "That is the serial killer that escaped and was later killed isn't it?"

Alex shook his head, "Yes, that is correct. By that time I had left the FBI, but was called in to consult on the case. Since then I have consulted on four other cases, but I spend most of my time studying and writing about serial killers."

"I must warn you that Sheriff Riley isn't too keen on asking for outside help."

Alex stopped and looked at her, "You wouldn't be asking for outside help, you would be letting me assist you in finding this killer. This is the perfect opportunity to study a serial killer who has no intention of stopping. If I am correct in my assumptions, this killer has struck before and when he is done here he will move on to another unsuspecting town."

Melancon looked at him closely. He was confirming her greatest fears, "I have run this case through VICAP and came up empty handed. I sent out requests to as many law enforcement agencies as I could, thinking the same thing. So far no one has responded."

Alex informed her, "When David Thorguson escaped we sent out requests to the various coroners' offices as well. That is where we struck pay dirt. One of the coroners remembered working a case with our similarities and called the case in."

Melancon was impressed. She hadn't thought about that. Dr. Harrison could help them contacting his colleagues. "I will get right on that. Our coroner mentioned that our guy showed no hesitation marks when killing the victims, which leads me to believe this isn't his first rodeo."

Alex informed Detective Melancon, "Another possibility is that he has been doing this for a while, but instead of displaying the first bodies he buried them."

"We just had a serial killer here that was dumping the bodies into the bayou. From the sheer number of bodies he had been doing it for a while."

"That was the Carl Ledet case, correct?"

Melancon nodded her head, "Yes, but unfortunately we can't ask him. However, if his journals are correct, then the bodies we recovered were from his handiwork. Right now I have our computer technicians doing background checks on any newcomers."

"That may work, but if he has done this before he has been extremely careful. You want to look at anyone who has never had a record. I mean this person will be so squeaky clean that there won't even be a speeding ticket on his record. Plus, he needs somewhere away from town and prying eyes to kill these victims. That is, unless he is killing the victims on the spot."

Melancon informed him, "Two were killed on the scene, but the others were taken to a different location before being staged." Jo thought about Bill Collins and the plantation home he'd bought. She tried to remember any more plantation homes, etc. that had been purchased recently and drew a blank, but the local realtor would know.

Melancon informed Alex, "I will get with the local realtor here. She should be in around nine o'clock. If anyone will know, it is her. Even if she didn't sell the piece of property she would keep track of any recent sales in the area."

Melancon opened an office door, "Sheriff Riley this is Alex Hamilton, the profiler Officer Diaz mentioned."

Sheriff Riley stood up and shook Alex's hand. "Nice to meet you." Sheriff Riley was still skeptical that this wasn't Mayor Daigle's handiwork. He wouldn't put it past the man to go behind his back. He would see how this played out. He did not believe in miracles, but if this man was here to help, it would be a miracle.

Sheriff Riley made further introductions, "You already met Detective Jo Melancon. This is her partner, Detective Chad Picou."

Detective Picou stood up and shook his hand. "You helped capture the serial killer in Hope, Louisiana didn't you?"

Before Alex could answer, another man stood up and introduced himself, "It is a pleasure to meet you sir. I am Mayor Daigle. We sure are happy that you have offered your assistance."

Alex looked at the mayor through guarded eyes. He could sense the tension in the room. "Thank you, sir. From what Detective Melancon has been telling me you are close to catching this man. If I can be of any assistance in speeding this along I am more than willing to offer my expertise."

Detective Picou spoke up, "So you are no longer with the FBI and are offering your services free of charge?"

Alex shook his head, "I know it sounds too good to be true, but I am being honest. I am going by what I read in the papers, but this may be a win win situation for all of us."

Alex continued, "What I would like to do is see your file and offer you a profile of this individual. If I am correct in my assumption, once he is finished here, he will move on and continue in another city. I don't think this is his first time at killing and he has no intention of being caught."

Picou agreed, "So far there have been no hesitation marks on the bodies. We are dealing with religious killings. He has been leaving us notes letting us know that these victims were sinners. Even though the bodies were in gruesome shape, I believe he showed great restraint. He was very attentive to details, leaving no trace evidence behind."

"I believe you are on the right path in finding this killer. He does not choose his victims at random. These killings are personal to him. He has chosen these individuals to expose their sins. There is a possibility that he knew his victims and knew them well."

Picou agreed, "He knew these people better than anyone else. Everyone was surprised, even the spouses, when the victims' sins were revealed."

Alex went on to state, "Your killer more than likely believes he is saving their soul from eternal damnation."

Sheriff Riley stepped in, "Murders like this are rare here. If you are sincere in your offer to help us catch this guy, I am more than happy to welcome you to our town. I can honestly say though that I am surprised."

Alex laughed, "My wife warned me I may have a hard time convincing you that I really just want to help. I know that some FBI agents have put a bad taste in a few mouths, but trust me, we are not all bad. Some of us out there do want to catch the bad guys and aren't worried about the glory that goes with it. I have no problem hiding in the shadows and helping you catch him. There is a catch though; I would like to study this killer.”

Sheriff Riley knew there would be a catch, but he didn’t fully comprehend, “What do you mean study this killer?”

Alex ran his hands through his hair, trying to figure out the best way to approach this, “This type of serial killer is one that I have only studied about. I have never met one up close and personal. If we catch him, I would like to learn more from him so that I can add it to my arsenal.”

“That’s all you want? What all is involved in studying him?”

“After he is caught and arraigned I would ask the District Attorney about conducting some personal interviews, to find out what makes this killer tick.”

Sheriff Riley ran his fingers along his jawline, “I don’t see where that would be a problem. When I have a chance I will call the DA so that y’all can talk face to face.”

Alex informed him, “There is plenty of time for that. Right now, I want to get started on this profile. I know the detectives are busy and don’t have time to answer questions, but if I could at least review the file.”

Sheriff Riley nodded his head, “We would be grateful for any help you can give us. You will receive full cooperation from the detectives and officers working the case.” The Sheriff gave a telling glance to Picou and Melancon. They both nodded their heads in agreement. They all wanted the same thing, this guy behind bars, or six feet under, just as long as he was stopped.

Alex knew what they were looking for. He also wanted some of the same answers. They needed an expert opinion as to why this man killed. They needed to know what drove him emotionally. How he thought, how he felt. That may be the only way to find him. As of now, he had eluded detection and left no evidence at the scenes.

Picou responded, "I was just getting ready to go over the files myself. Melancon went to call the real estate agent and coroners like you suggested. If there is anything you need to know, please don't hesitate to ask. "

Alex stated, "All right then, why don't we go somewhere so you can give me a briefing on what you know so far."

Picou showed Alex to the conference room where they had everything laid out, "As you can see from the boards he has killed six victims."

Alex studied the gruesome photos. He noticed that victim number two was only drowned, no mutilation on his body. "Why did he stray with victim number two?"

"From what we can gather Eric Devareaux, victim number two, was a paranoid man. The security on his house was tighter than at Fort Knox. If our killer tried to get near with a vehicle there were enough alarms to announce his arrival from any direction he came. Devareaux had motion sensors all around the area. Even though our killer stalked Devareaux and knew about the alarm system, he did not know Devareaux was too cheap to have it linked to the sheriff's office. The only thing that happened when the alarm was tripped was that it notified Devareaux. If he had known then he may have stayed a while with the body. As it stood, he was in and out of there. He watched Devareaux drown, left the note and then took off. He kept his face turned away from the cameras at all times. The only thing we know is a general build. He dressed in black and kept a hood over his head and face."

"So your guy had knowledge of their lifestyles, but was not privy to all the details."

Picou nodded his head, "That is our general understanding for now. It may be wrong, but it fits what we know. Going by the notes left behind at each scene, he believes they were guilty of the seven deadly sins. Eric Devareaux was consumed by greed. Our first victim, Victoria Russo, knew her husband was having an affair, but put money above all else. Her friends confirmed that she took pride in the fact that she could spend as much money as she wanted and her husband just went along with it."

Alex interrupted, "Let me guess she was guilty of pride?"

"Yes. The third victim, Graham Easterly, not only beat his wife, but he had a mistress as well. Mr. Easterly's body was found on the doorstep of his mistress. Now, according to his wife, she told absolutely no one except for her therapist that her husband beat her, she was too ashamed. She did not know he was cheating on her until after his death."

Alex asked, "So how did this guy know that the victim was beating his wife, and had a mistress?"

"That is what we are trying to figure out. The best we can come up with is that the killer must have seen the bruises on Mrs. Easterly and pieced it together. Mrs. Easterly thought she was good at hiding the bruises, but Melancon saw them right away."

Alex pondered everything the detective just told him, "So Easterly was guilty of wrath I take it?"

Picou agreed, "Yes. The fourth victim was a local food critic, Brian LeBlanc. From looking at him, you would never know it, but his note read gluttony. The fifth victim, Pam Benoit, was considered lazy and everyone in town had no qualms confirming it. She was probably an easy choice for sloth. The latest victim was a surprise to us, as well as her husband. Turns out she had been having affairs with several men while her husband was at work. Grace Aucoin was found guilty of lust."

Alex took the information in, "So most of these victims hid their sins really well is what you are telling me?"

"Yes. It came as quite a surprise to everyone here. Whoever is doing this somehow knew the deep, dark secrets of the people in this town. We just can't figure out how. These victims must have talked to someone, but since they aren't alive to tell us we are trying to piece it all together."

Alex asked, "So how did the killer get close enough to Devareaux to drug him?"

"Our killer is smart. He found out what Eric Devareaux liked to drink and sent him a gift-wrapped bottle that had ketamine in it. The tox screen came back and there were enough sedatives in there to kill a horse."

"I thought those bottles were tamper proof."

Picou informed him, "The secretary who signed for the basket made the comment that she thought the wax on the bottle looked funny, but Devareaux didn't heed her warning. He told her it was more than likely a mistake made at the factory and he would bring it home to enjoy."

"So this guy was careful and meticulous. These murders are definitely premeditated."

Picou agreed, "Yes, our first victim was killed when her husband was out of town with his mistress. Although from what I understand everyone in town knew Mr. Russo was going to be gone that night."

Alex stepped over to the board and studied the photos more intently, "So all that remains is envy?"

"Yes. With each note, he has stated which sin they were guilty of, but it is proving it. I want to make sure he isn't trying to throw us off. He was sloppy at this last scene, but he didn't count on our crime scene techs taking the initiative and searching the drains. He probably figured he was safe killing her in a hotel room where there were more than likely to be thousands of prints and various degrees of misleading evidence."

Alex found this interesting, "So now you have DNA evidence on the killer?"

"Yes, no matches, but when we catch the guy we have enough to place him at the scene of the crime."

Alex asked, "Was the same drug used in all murders?"

"Yes, Special 'K' was used in all six murders."

Alex let out a sigh, "That is easy to buy on the streets, so that may be difficult to track down."

"I've asked the local drug dealers here, but no one here is into that. Around here the high ticket items are anything cheap that can get the kids high."

Alex suggested, "So he has to go out of town or online to purchase the drugs."

"That is how it looks. From the precision of the cuts, it looks like our killer has a medical background or is very experienced with a knife."

Alex asked, "And none of the bodies had defensive wounds?"

"No. He may have had them sedated or stunned before they knew what was happening."

Alex pondered this for a moment, "I don't think these killings are random. He plans out each of his kills in an orderly fashion."

Picou agreed, "That is my assumption."

"Would it be possible to review the files so I can give you a more in depth profile?"

"Do you want to use the conference room? Everything is in there. If you need privacy I can go help Melancon and answer some emails."

Alex informed him, "I don't need privacy. I know how bad you want to catch this guy. I'll try to stay out of your way."

"Much appreciated."

As Alex read over the files, he became even more engrossed. Reading the reports sent a chill down his spine, but he was fascinated at the same time. How was he choosing these victims? How did he know that these victims were guilty of a sin? Was he stalking or did he already know them? Was that why there were no defensive wounds, because they knew their killer?

He had committed six killings without making a single mistake. This killer was highly organized and methodical. There was no refuting the man was disturbed and dangerous.

Towards the end of the day, Alex was comfortable with his profile. He gathered everyone in the conference room. "I have the beginnings of your profile. I will work on it some more, but just in case you have a suspect that fits I wanted to throw out there what I have so far. We are looking for a white male in his mid-thirties. He is a loner, but has a successful career. He is more than likely self-employed so he can control his time, but he may work in a small business where he won't be missed if he wasn't around the office for long periods of time. He is physically fit and well built. He is highly intelligent and well organized. He is borderline obsessive compulsive. This man has a lot of hidden rage, but controls it in public. He comes off as friendly or maybe even overly shy, but that is to hide his all-consuming anger. He believes he is on a mission from God and won't stop until that mission is completed. However, after he kills his last sinner there is a chance he will move on. There is also a chance he will wait until things cool down and begin again here. In his mind, he believes God is talking to him, telling him to do these things—maybe for some sort of reward.

He only renders them unconscious enough to manhandle them. I believe they were alive for the torture and killing. He needs them to understand why he is doing this and more than likely he wants to hear them confess to their sins."

Chapter 51

Melancon sat at her desk thinking about the day's developments. Only two plantations were bought over the last year. The rest of the real estate sales were in town. The first plantation was bought by the new chiropractor in town and he had been steadily renovating it, especially recently. Laura Miller also mentioned a conversation she had recently with Samuel Cheramie about possibly selling it now that it was almost renovated. That caught Melancon's attention.

Bill Collins bought the other plantation. Melancon knew about his purchase though. He had talked about it while at her house one night. Out of curiosity one day, she had even driven out there to check it out. She noticed that it also looked as if he had been busy with renovations. She just couldn't accept that Bill could be their killer. Although it would answer a lot of questions, especially how he knew so much about the murders.

Now, Samuel Cheramie she wasn't so sure about. She had never met the man. She sent an email to Officer Diaz to see if he could dig deeper into each man's backgrounds. Both men were new to the area, although Bill was originally from here.

She gnawed on her bottom lip as she considered the possibility that either man was their guy.

As she considered stopping for the day she heard the fax machine ring. Out of curiosity, she headed over to see what could be coming through at this hour. Her heart pounded in her ears as she read the fax, not believing what her eyes saw. She immediately picked up her phone and called Picou, "Where are you?"

Picou responded, "I'm on my way home. Why, please don't tell me we have another body."

"Get your ass back over here now. Do you know how to get in touch with Alex Hamilton?"

Picou responded, "Yeah, I have his number somewhere on my desk. Why, what is going on?"

"I finally got a response from my inquiries on unsolved murders. Turns out a little town not far from Alexandria, Louisiana had seven unsolved murders almost two years ago. Mon ami, the MO is a lot like ours, except the guy drowned the victims. There was no mutilation. It looks as if he may be escalating."

Picou let out a whistle, "Holy crap. I'm turning around right now. Did they say if they had any suspects?"

As Melancon answered, she scoured Picou's desk for Alex's phone number, "Mais non, but I'm calling Officer Diaz back in right now. I have two potential suspects he could pull up backgrounds on. If either of these two men lived there, then we may have the SOB."

As soon as she hung up with Picou she called Alex Hamilton, "Sir, I hate to call you this late, but are you on your way back to Hope?"

"Actually, I have a room here for the night. Do you need me for something?"

Melancon informed him, "Well, sir, I thought you would like to know that I just received a fax from a town up in central Louisiana that had seven unsolved murders, dating back almost two years ago. I was going to call Officer Diaz back in to see if he can do a background check on two possible suspects I obtained from talking to the real estate agent. There have only been two plantations purchased in the last year. The rest of the real estate sales were in town. We may actually have a suspect to order DNA samples from."

Alex felt that rush of adrenaline when a killer was about to be found, "I'm on my way back in."

Next Melancon called Officer Diaz, "I hate to bother you, but I need you back in the office as soon as possible."

He informed her, "I never left. I already got your message and started background checks."

Melancon asked, "Can you please see if any of the two men lived up in central Louisiana two years ago? I need to find out if they lived anywhere near Alexandria."

"I'll get right on it. It shouldn't take that long."

Melancon hoped the killer didn't plan to murder his next victim tonight. If the detective who had worked the other cases had entered those cases into VICAP then they may have caught this killer sooner. She had been checking VICAP daily and only recently sent out faxes to every law enforcement agency she could. It looked as if her efforts were about to pay off. She was thankful that they at least answered the fax.

Chapter 52
Envy

Envy ran deep through the very being of Matthew Watson.
This man had been competitive his whole life, whether it be
in sports, school or now in work and life. He had always
wanted to be the better person, whether he did that by
honesty or deceit. He craved praise. His achievements
were useless unless he received recognition for it. It was
nothing for him to steal the thunder away from one of his
co-workers and make sure he took the credit for a job well
done, whether he did anything or not.

Matthew did not take it well when one of his friends or co-
workers enjoyed the success he so badly craved. He sulked
and did everything in his power to make that person look
bad. He found a way to overturn that person's success. His
heart was as cold as ice.

Matthew had heard rumors that the current vice president
of Comeaux Construction was retiring. He became
extremely upset when he heard that Blake Savoie was up
for the promotion and not him. He had been with this
company longer and should be the one promoted and not
some newcomer who had not put in the time and dealt with
Jason Comeaux's idiocracies.

He realized that the only way to get that position was to get
rid of Blake Savoie. It was so easy to poison his name
around the office. The place was like a rumor mill and once
you said one thing about someone, it blew way out of
proportion. A few negative comments and Blake and the

whole office had their tongues wagging. It didn't matter to Matthew if Blake's wife may leave him over the rumors he spread. All that mattered to Matthew was that he got the job and not Blake Savoie.

When he heard the rumors, he could not believe the man would do such a thing. Jason Comeaux and others should be appalled at themselves for believing such vicious rumors. More importantly, Matthew Watson should be ashamed of himself for doing something so vile. He should never be that envious of someone as to ruin their livelihood. After all, envy was one of the seven deadly sins. It could be such a malicious emotion. Envy was the all- consuming desire to possess what others had. Envy was the ulcer of the human soul.

It had become a way of life for Matthew Watson. He coveted thy neighbors and friend's charmed life. His envy was an obsession and he had committed vile grievances in the name of it.

Matthew Watson coveted the possessions of those around him. He would lie, cheat, and steal to get what he obsessed over. His envy drove him to commit these sins.

He was still at work, or acting as if he was working late. He had figured out this sinner's trick. He deceived those around him. While everyone thought he was busy working, he was planting more seeds of lies. This man was truly malicious.

He feared the police were moving in to arrest him so he had no time to wait. He must set this soul free and move on. He could not risk getting caught this close to completing his mission. He did not want to see his mother's soul banished in purgatory forever. He thought he was being careful and that God would make sure he completed his mission. He did not count on the tenacity of the detectives. He thought for sure that they would understand the meaning behind the notes. He had been so wrong.

He watched as Matthew stepped out of the office building and walked right towards him. The parking lot was now empty. He watched as the sinner picked up his pace, as if he was eager to atone for his sins.

For weeks, he had been praying for this man. Praying for him to stop his hateful ways and correct the wrongs he had done. Instead, he fell deeper into sin, letting envy take over his thoughts. Now his soul must be cleansed. This was the last sinner. Surely, after this one God would release his mother from purgatory.

This was the moment when the sinner's forgiveness was almost at hand. He was only an instrument of God's will. He continued to pray for the man's soul as the sinner moved closer to his salvation.

He moved swiftly, being merciful when he stunned him with the Taser gun. The sinner had no time to react, only letting out a soft gasp as he crumpled to the ground.

He slapped Matthew across the face several times to wake him up. He was still very groggy. When he went to defend the assault on him, he realized he couldn't move his arms or legs, they were restrained to a table.

A cold dread came across him. He heard someone ask, "Are you ready to atone for your sins?"

Matthew wondered what this maniac was talking about. How long had he been here? He felt the knife blade slice into his shoulder. "Please…"

His captor sneered down at him, "You must confess to the Almighty God all of your sins."

***

Matthew begged and pleaded for the man to stop. The pain in his shoulder was intense. The slushing noise the knife made as it was removed from his flesh made him queasy. He felt the knife graze his body. He shuddered at the thought of it entering him again.

His captor plunged the knife into his upper thigh, dragging the blade down. He watched in horror as he wrenched the blade, cutting through flesh and muscle in one long stroke. Matthew let out a horrific scream.

Fear ate at his gut. This man was going to kill him. He felt the knife blade rip into his gut as white-hot pain enveloped him. He wondered how much longer he would be tortured. He had learned one thing, time really did stand still in hell.

Matthew closed his eyes tight. He could not stand to look at all the blood, his blood. The pungent, coppery smell was thick and heavy in the room. He gagged at the overwhelming smell.

***

The sinner started to black out once again. He needed to confess to his sins so that he could be cleansed, "You need to confess to Almighty God so I can set you free."

The evil in this sinner was strong, challenging him. He
refused to atone for his sins. He should have known
Matthew would be stubborn. He'd learned a lot about him
over the last couple of days. He knew that he believed he
did no wrong. That was part of the problem with envy. You
could never admit when you were wrong and when you
had what you wanted it was never enough.

He looked down at the dead body in disgust. He recited as
God instructed, "Dominus vobiscum." Slowly he ran his
thumb over the sinner's forehead, chin, and chest in the
sign of the cross to give him absolution.

He headed to the bathroom to clean up before he disposed
of the body. Not bothering with the bathroom light, he
turned on the shower and stepped into the warm water.
He lathered his body several times until he was positive he
had washed the blood off of him.

Once the smell of blood no longer lingered, he turned off
the water and stepped out of the tub. He quickly dressed so
that he could stage the body before daybreak. He only had
a short time remaining. This would be Matthew's final day
at work. Now the wrongs he had done could be righted.
His envy would no longer ruin lives.

Chapter 53

Melancon took in a deep breath, almost gagging on the smell of death. She stared at the body lying spread eagle on the front steps of Comeaux Construction. The dead man's eyes stared back at her, begging her to find his killer. She wished they had put together the pieces and saved at least one of the victim's from this horrendous death but they were too late.

The body was mutilated almost beyond recognition. She yanked her gaze away. She was letting her feelings get in the way. At least they had a name for their killer. At this very moment, Detective Picou was leading the SWAT team to his house for an arrest. She wanted to be there for the arrest, but someone needed to stay and process the scene.

She observed the growing crowd. Everyone was curious to see what happened. Melancon instructed one of the officers to push the crowd further back to keep them from looking at the body.

The crime scene photographer was busy taking pictures of what she hoped to be their last victim. Melancon prayed that Picou made an arrest today.

The poor man that stumbled upon the body was still white from shock. This would be something the man never forgot.

Chapter 54

Picou looked over at Officer Diaz and nodded his head. The old plantation home was massive and they had no idea if he was here or at work. With it still morning, they figured he had gone to the office, but when they arrived there, they didn't find him.

Picou prayed to God that they didn't waste precious time and he left town. The For Sale sign out front confirmed their worst fears; he had planned to leave town when the last murder was completed.

His vehicle was still out back, but that didn't mean he didn't have another means of leaving town. When they obtained the warrant to search his financial records they discovered he had a large bank account and more than enough money to leave town.

From what they discovered so far, he had made plans to start a life in another city, another small town in Louisiana where he would probably start killing again.

They searched the house from top to bottom and didn't find him. From the kitchen window, Picou noticed several workshops out back and thought he may be hiding out there. He instructed Officer Diaz, "Let's split up in groups of two and see if our guy is hiding in one of the workshops out back."

"Yes, sir."

Officer Diaz and Picou took the smokehouse. The smell of bleach hit them before they even opened the door. This was where the killings took place and he was trying to erase the evidence before he left. Picou held up his fingers and counted down from three. Officer Diaz kicked the door in. They found Samuel Cheramie on his knees.

He held his hands up, "God told me you would find me." He picked up his gun and aimed it directly at Picou, "I can't let you take me in though. God told me once my mission was complete that my mother's soul would be set free, but my mission isn't complete. She is still in purgatory. I must move on and finish my mission. You must let me."

Alex had been right; his mother's death had been the stressor. He must have had a mental breakdown when she committed suicide. The young priest's denial to allow her body to pass through the church had been more than the man's psyche could handle and he broke. After the first fax came back several more followed. They all wanted to talk to Samuel Cheramie.

Picou shook his head, "I can't let you escape Samuel. What you did is against the law."

He sneered at Picou, "Maybe against man's law, but not God's."

Picou replied, "Killing is a sin as well."

Samuel shook his head, "No, God talked to me. He chose me for this mission. These people committed the most atrocious of sins. I have to free my mother from purgatory. It has to be a life for a life. They were holy sacrifices."

Picou watched as Samuel's hands shook. He kept his gun on him. "Samuel you need to drop the gun. It is over son."

Samuel shook his head, "I can't stop. My mission isn't complete yet. God still hasn't released my mother's soul. Look for yourself. She is still right here."

Samuel, never dropping his gun, moved to the side to allow the detective to see the glass coffin that held his mother's body. The man cried as he explained, "The church wouldn't let me bury her in the mausoleum. She committed a mortal sin by committing suicide. The priest refused to listen to me when I tried to explain that cancer had killed her. She couldn't take the pain anymore. I couldn't just bury her in the backyard. God came to me that night and gave me a mission to complete. After every death, I waited to see if her soul had been set free, but there are so many sinners in the world. I fear that she will never find absolution."

Picou tried to reason with the man, "Samuel all that remains of your mother is bones. Her soul is free."

"No! You lie! I can see her soul trapped in her body, waiting to be set free. It's not fair that these other sinners have been cleansed, God has forgiven them."

Picou tried to reason with him one more time, "Samuel put the gun down. Let's go talk to Father Wagoner. If you explain to him about the cancer and your mother's death, he will absolve her of her sins."

Samuel looked at him, "Do you think so?"

"First, you have to put down the gun Samuel."

Slowly Samuel eased the gun to the floor. He looked at his mother's body one more time. "I am doing this for you mother. Maybe I will find you absolution."

For just a moment, Picou swore he saw a tear fall from the corpse's eye socket. It had to be his imagination, though. "Samuel I need to cuff you. I will keep my promise, though, and ask Father Wagoner to come talk to you. I will also ask that he come and absolve your mother of her sins. We will make sure that she receives a proper burial."

"Maybe you are the one God told me about. The one that will take care of everything."

As Picou led the man out to the patrol car, he wondered if any of this would have happened if the priest had allowed his mother a proper church burial.

As he watched the police cruiser pull away with Samuel, he called Melancon, "We got him. It's over."

"Thank the Lord."

Picou informed her, "It may be a while before we can close the case though. I need to ask a priest for a favor. Alex was right in his assumption that his mother's death sent him over the edge. His mother's corpse is in the old smokehouse where he committed the murders. He has her in a glass coffin."

Melancon let out a whistle, "That's a new one."

"Are you finished with the crime scene?"

"Yes, I am getting ready to head to the office and finalize my report."

Picou informed her, "I am going to go surprise my wife."

Melancon let out a laugh, "I am sure she would be more than happy to see you."

Before Picou headed to the bakery to see Mia, he called Gwen at the travel agency. "Gwen, you know that cruise I have been talking to you about?"

Gwen asked, "Don't tell me. You are ready to purchase those tickets."

Picou smiled from ear to ear, "Would you please have something ready for me to pick up? I want to surprise Mia with it this afternoon when I walk into the bakery."

"I'll print you out the itinerary."

"That will be perfect. I should be there in about half an hour." Picou informed the crime scene techs that he was leaving them in charge, "I am going to go see my wife and tell her we can finally take our honeymoon."

Chapter 55

Mia saw Chad walk into the bakery with a bouquet of flowers and a gift-wrapped box. "I am guessing the arrest went well."

Instead of answering her, he took her in his arms and gave her a deep kiss. He handed her the flowers, "These are for my lovely wife who has had to put up with quite a bit lately."

He handed her the gift-wrapped box, "I wanted to surprise you with something since we never had a honeymoon."

"You didn't have to get me anything. I never even missed having a honeymoon. All I wanted was to become Mrs. Chad Picou."

"Well Mrs. Chad Picou, open your gift?"

Mia tore open the package and looked inside, "It's an itinerary."

"I figured now that the case was over, we could take that honeymoon you dreamed of."

Mia looked at Chad impishly, "I would love to go on a cruise with you or any other place, but I hope we can change the dates."

"Do you want me to ask Gwen to pick something else? I just figured you would love a cruise. It was all you talked about for the longest time."

Mia whispered in his ear, "I'm pregnant."

Chad picked her up and swung her, "Are you sure?"

She nodded, "I had my first doctor's appointment this morning. I am eight weeks along. I am having a hard time on dry land and don't think the sea will be any better on my stomach. Something tells me that neither of us would have a pleasant time on a boat."

"I'll be damned. I'm going to be a father."

Chad didn't think he could be any happier than he was right now. "Have you told your parents?"

"I thought we could tell them after this case was over."

"I say we go tell them right now."

Mia tried to slow him down, "Let's go home for a while. We can tell them when they come over for supper tonight."

Chad pulled her into his arms one more time to kiss her. If they were at home, he knew he wouldn't stop kissing her, "Let's go home."

"I'll be right behind you."

Chapter 56

Jo had just made it home when her doorbell rang. She had half a mind not to answer it. Everyone who saw her wanted to ask her about today and if it was true that Samuel Cheramie had been arrested.

Looking through the peephole, she saw Bill waiting for her, "I almost didn't answer the door. I thought you were another curious neighbor wanting to know if it was true about Samuel Cheramie."

Bill never even answered her. Instead, he pulled her into his arms and kissed her passionately. "You have no idea how long I have wanted to do that."

Jo had a hard time catching her breath, "So what stopped you?"

"I didn't want to get involved while you were in the middle of a homicide investigation. I wanted you to know when I slept with you that it was because of you and not to get information on the case."

Jo kissed him back, "I don't think I would have even considered that, but I am glad you find me attractive. I was beginning to think that there was something wrong with me."

Bill brought her inside and closed the door, "Do you want me to call and order a pizza?"

She wrapped her arms around his neck, "I'm not hungry for food right now."

Nuzzling at her neck, "Good neither am I."

Bill gazed her body up and down, with desire showing in his eyes. Jo pulled him closer to her, reveling in the feel of him.

His hands slowly worked her blouse out from under her slacks. His hands felt warm against the bare skin of her back. She let out a moan in pleasure.

His hands made their way up to her breasts and cupped them through her bra. Growing dizzy with desire, she held onto his shoulders for support, slowly wrapping her arms around his neck. She breathed in the scent of him, musky, earthy, spicy, and completely male. He was intoxicating.

Her nipples grew taut, begging to be touched. His hands expertly unclasped her bra allowing her breasts to spill out.

He pinched one nipple and then the next. She wanted him inside of her. Jo wasn't sure how much longer she could take this torturous pleasure.

Bill scooped her up and carried her off to her bedroom. He laid her on the bed and removed her slacks and panties.

He looked down at her beautiful naked body and desire coiled through him. Heat burst through his body, warming his blood. He wanted to savor every inch of her magnificent body, to taste and breathe in her feminine scent. His groin twitched in anticipation.

He took in the sight of her voluptuous breasts. They were perfect mounds for her body. Her nipples were taut, begging to be touched and suckled.

His gaze roamed further down her body to her narrow waist, flat stomach, and long legs. She had the kind of legs that were made to wrap around a man.

His voice gruff with need, Bill whispered in her ear, "I'm not sure how much longer I can wait. I've wanted you for so long."

"I need you now."

That was all the encouragement he needed. In one swift movement, he completely filled her. He found his rhythm quickly. It was fast and urgent. Every thrust took her breath away, bringing her closer to another mind shattering orgasm. She matched his rhythm, meeting each thrust as they became faster and faster.

Epilogue

Father Scott Wagoner stood over the coffin of Bertha Cheramie and prayed. "God, our Father, Your power brought us to birth, Your providence guided our lives, and by Your command we return to dust…"

Chad and Mia Picou stood on one side of Samuel Cheramie while Jo Melancon and Bill Collins stood along the other side of the prisoner. Samuel Cheramie made a deal with the District Attorney. He would plead guilty of murder if he could be given a brief reprieve to attend his mother's funeral service. That saved the state a lot of money on his trial, even though they had more than enough evidence against him. Samuel, under heavy guard, stood forlorn as he watched his mother finally laid to rest.

It had taken some fancy talking for Father Wagoner to agree to perform the funeral rites. He finished the service with, "May almighty God have mercy on you, forgive you your sins, and lead you to everlasting life. May the almighty and merciful Lord grant you pardon, absolution, and remission of your sins. May our Lord Jesus Christ absolve you. I, by His authority, release you from every bond of excommunication and interdict, as I am empowered and you have a need. Now, I absolve you from your sins. In the name of the Father, and of the Son, and of the Holy Spirit."

As the body was lowered and dirt scattered along the glass coffin a chill rushed through Chad. For a moment, he swore that he saw the soul of Bertha Cheramie rise from the ground and hover over the gravesite. Even more chilling was that Samuel must have seen the same thing because he looked at Chad with tears in his eyes, "Thank you Detective Picou. She is finally at rest."

Thank you!

Dear Reader,

Thank you for purchasing this book. I hope you enjoyed reading this novel as much as I enjoyed writing it.

It is very important for me to hear what you think about the book. Your reviews give me inspiration in my future writings. You can leave a review on Amazon, Goodreads or Barnes and Noble.

Your thoughts and opinions mean a lot to me.

Please enjoy a sample of A Kiss So Deadly. The ghosts of Marquette Plantation must warn Bridgette that evil lurks in the shadows. All that is not as it seems. She may be falling in love with the wrong man.

Also, be sure to check out my website and social media sites for upcoming books and giveaways.

Sincerely,

Mary Theriot

Links

Website www.maryreasontheriot.com

Goodreads for reviews,

http://www.goodreads.com/MaryReasonTheriot

Facebook,

http://goo.gl/Sd0VgY

Twitter - @Mktheriot

Google+ - +MaryTheriot

YouTube

http://goo.gl/ErM1M6

Pinterest

http://www.pinterest.com/mktheriot

Blog Page, www.maryreasontheriot.me

A Kiss So Deadly

By: Mary Reason Theriot

Marquette Plantation was, and still is, a relatively modest Louisiana plantation. The Marquette family has owned the land since 1767. It has withstood the years, and showed the well-earned prosperity by those who worked here. Pierre Marquette knew how to work it and accumulated his wealth by planting rice, among other local crops.

Pierre refused to allow anything to come between him and his dream. He quickly learned how to irrigate from the bayou waters. They feasted off the ducks and geese that flocked to the rice fields to eat. When the high waters would force them from their land, they camped out on the levees. In addition, once the waters receded, there was an abundance of crawfish, frogs, and catfish.

One unfortunate year, it took three months for the water to recede. Even though they lost almost everything they owned, at least they still had their home. This time, they realized the need to build the buildings off the ground to protect their dwellings from the water. When Pierre had acquired the two thousand acres, hundreds of them had pine and cypress trees that needed to be cleared. Being a shrewd businessman, he started a profitable lumber and sawmill business, as well as farming the land.

Before Pierre built the massive plantation, he and Genevieve lived in a small home with the other Acadians who traveled and settled here with them. It took him several years to build Genevieve her dream home. Unfortunately, she only lived there for a short while before her passing. Yellow fever hit the area with a vengeance and took many lives, including hers.

Before Genevieve's death, she and Pierre would sit on the veranda to enjoy a cup of coffee before he headed out to the fields. Genevieve's untimely passing left Pierre heartbroken and unsure of what to do with the children she left behind in his charge. Genevieve's sister, a spinster, had helped in the kitchen and with the children before Genevieve's passing. He missed her dearly, but as a widower, it did not look right for two single adults to live under one roof together. Besides, he needed help desperately with the children. His children were a raucous lot and lost without their dear mother. He wed her only days after his beloved wife's death.

Looking around, Genevieve was proud of her descendants. Despite the ravages of war, storms, and hard times, this plantation maintained many of their traditions as well as their French language. She beamed with pride as Bridgette strived to educate people of their unique cultural identity, forged by some four centuries of turbulent history.

Chapter 1
The Life of Pierre and Genevieve Marquette

In 1750, despite the savage war that raged all around
Acadia, Genevieve's ancestors desperately tried to make a
life for themselves here in Nova Scotia. The small
settlement of Acadia consisted of peasants, fishermen, and
farmers.

Most of the settlers originated from the northwest
provinces of France. They came to the New World to make
a better life for themselves. All they desired was a place to
live in peace and raise a family. The ground was fertile here
and, despite the harsh weather, they managed to flourish.
Most of the Acadians ignored the newcomers moving in and
went on with their lives. With the fighting over, perhaps
they would find peace.

Genevieve had been born here in Acadia and knew no other
way of life. Her mother taught her well. She knew how to
keep a clean house and spin cloth. At the tender age of
fourteen, Genevieve met the love of her life, Pierre
Marquette. She didn't care that he was ten years her senior.
He swept her off her feet. No other man could make her
feel the way Pierre Marquette did. When he spoke, his
voice was the only voice she heard. When Pierre talked to
her, she saw the twinkle in his eyes. Time stood still when
he was near her.

At six-foot four, he was one of the tallest men in Acadia. His
arms were rippled with muscles; his body lean and tan from
hard work. It may have been scandalous, but she
daydreamed about what he looked like without a shirt.

Her wedding day had been one of the happiest days of her
life. She wore an ivory satin dress, and Pierre wore his best
suit. The sun shined through the stained glass windows,
sending prisms of color dancing all around the small church.
Fragrant fresh flowers from her mama's garden filled the
church to make this the perfect day.

When they married, Pierre's family helped them build a sturdy, well-made house. Even in the coldest of winters, it kept them warm. After the harsh winters, lovely springs and warm summers always came. The rich earth came to life and produced bountiful crops.

Tall pine trees and sporadic bunches of wildflowers grew in patches around the house. Genevieve found several rose bushes growing wild in the woods and transplanted them in her flower beds. With the help of Pierre's green thumb, they thrived.

Whatever her new husband raised flourished. Their apple orchard was bountiful, as were the vegetable crops, the most successful crop was potatoes. He built dykes along the land to protect the crops from the flooding of the fluctuating tides.

With the money he earned from his crops, he purchased extra cattle that grew fat, this allowed them enough milk to barter. He raised pigs to use for lard and meat. They worked hard, but it was a good life.

Genevieve's favorite pastime was the couchon da lait, where Pierre roasted a whole pig. Friends and family came over for a fais do do. They played music, danced and drank.

While Pierre hunted, trapped, fished, and toiled the land to keep food on their table, Genevieve stayed home to tend to the household chores. She kept busy making candles, tending to cheeses, feeding chickens and gathering their eggs, and spinning cloth. The spinning wheel was a cherished gift from her parents and Genevieve spent her spare time making quilts and fine lace.

In 1755, Genevieve's perfect world was on the brink of ruin. England was at odds with the Acadians. The British authorities, in what is now known as Nova Scotia, wanted to expel the Acadians to prevent any alliance with the French. A war seemed imminent between the British and the French in North America.

Rumors spread about the Acadians being exiled by the British authorities. If the rumors were true, where would they go? What were they to do? Pierre had money saved, but what about their household goods? Everything they owned must be turned over to the British except for what they could carry on the ship. Worse, they would not be paid for anything the British confiscated. This couldn't be true, could it? It had to be just tongues wagging.

Pierre feared what the English would do once they were exiled. He did not trust them; he feared they would be deported and sent back to France. Late one night, Pierre woke Genevieve.

Pierre and several others had gathered what they could and planned to flee before it was too late. Pierre heard rumors of the French settling in a place called Louisiana. This may be their only chance. It would be a dangerous journey, but they might be facing far worse if they remained here.

It was a long, arduous trip to their new location. Several friends died along the way of illness or exposure. The Micmac Indian tribe helped them hide from the British, offering food and shelter along the way. Genevieve could never thank them enough for their generosity.

Each night they made camp, built a fire, and cooked a meal. The men hunted for wild game or caught fish along the way, and took turns keeping a lookout while the others slept. There were many dangers ahead of them, including unfriendly Indians, bears, and other dangerous animals. As they traveled south, they began to have problems with deadly snakes and alligators. When they arrived along the banks of the Mississippi, they found almost no civilization. They came across a few trading posts, villages, and forts. Now and then, they were welcomed, given fresh water and a place to rest. Unfortunately, in some places they were clearly not welcome. Whenever possible, they would find passage on a ship. Pierre attempted to keep their spirits high by reminding them that their ancestors forged a new life for themselves in Acadia and they could too.

Louisiana was more beautiful than Genevieve ever imagined. It was a picturesque sight with its drooping willow trees, rugged oak trees dripping with moss, and the cypress trees growing in the water. But, what excited her most was that she could talk to people in her own tongue.

The scenery of this land was wild, but on the banks of the bayous were fields and fields of corn, cotton, sugarcane, and rice. On either side of the bayou stood a curtain of moss draped swamplands that framed the imposing residences like none they had ever seen.

The tortuous waters of the bayou appeared glassy as they made their way further down south. Dusk illuminated the extraordinary splendor. She adored how she could see the inverted images of the broad spreading oak trees, and how the cypress trees were reminiscent of long motionless pendants. The descending sun brightened the tops of the trees as the sky turned into beautiful hues of crimsons and purples. She loved to watch as the white herons took flight against the hazy sky and how the alligators rippled the water. As much as she missed her home in Nova Scotia, she knew she would be happy here. As long as she had Pierre by her side, she had no need for anything else.

Even though they made it to Louisiana, their journey was far from over. Genevieve longed for a place to call home, and they still had to find somewhere to settle and raise their family. One where they could practice Catholicism without persecution. When they arrived in Louisiana, they found many Roman Catholics practicing their faith.

They also learned that all of Pierre's fears were confirmed; the Acadians had indeed been forced into exile. Families had been separated, forced to board ships for unknown lands. Some were forced to return to France, while others were sent to prisons in England, and still more were on their way down the coast aboard overcrowded ships. The British then burned their homes to prevent the exiled from returning.

It was disheartening to learn that the rumors were true and that they were forced to forfeit their lands, tenements, livestock, money, and household goods. How could one government be so cruel to citizens who only wanted to lead a peaceful, yet productive life? The English did not care if families remained together. They just wanted these Acadians exiled from their land.

While in New Orleans, Pierre learned that in other parishes, land was available for the taking. He firmly believed that those who owned property had power. It took him a while to acquire what he desired, but Genevieve never doubted him for one moment.

The ground was fertile here and Pierre could smell the rich soil to determine if they would have a good year or not. Just from the smell of the soil, he ascertained whether or not it was rich in nutrients.

They worked hard day in and day out. When it came time to harvest the rice, they would work in the fields from sun up to sun down.

Louisiana went from being under the control of the French government to the Spanish government, but all Pierre cared about was making a life for them. He welcomed any of his fellow brothers and allowed them to build homes here, all he asked in return was help working the crops.

They only had trouble one time; a young wife fell in love with her husband's best friend. Late one night, they decided to kill the husband so that they could be together. The wife informed the others in the settlement that he left in the middle of the night, no longer desiring to work the land. Months later when the land flooded, his body was discovered. By that time, she and the best friend had left, more than likely fearing that they would soon be discovered.

Pierre made the untamed land flourish; Marquette Plantation was now their home. They had a family and plenty of friends to share the good and bad times. Pierre, and those living here, had no concerns when the American Revolution broke out. That was between the American colonies and had nothing to do with Louisiana, until 1779 when Spain declared war upon England. With Louisiana being under Spanish control, Louisiana was brought into the war. Some of the Acadians saw this as an opportunity to fight back against the tyranny England imposed on them.

Genevieve enjoyed living here, although her time was brief. The climate was milder than in her beloved Acadia; there was no snow here and no freezing winters. Even the waters were abundant in food, carrying with them shrimp, oysters, crab, and fish. Unfortunately, everything Genevieve knew and loved was here, but just out of her grasp. This was where she died, and where she would spend all eternity. This was not a bad place to spend eternity, however. To her, nothing compared to the beauty of Marquette Plantation. It was especially beautiful at night, when the moonlight rippled along the bayou. She considered herself fortunate to watch her family prosper over the years.

She walked along the drive of the plantation, shaded by the oaks. After all these years, it was still a breathtaking place. Her descendants had kept up the property, so she had no doubt it was still the grandest plantation in all of Louisiana. She had asked that Pierre place the French doors where they could have a breeze that flowed through the house from the bayou. Even in the heat of summer, a cool breeze brought some welcome relief from the oppressive heat. Wraparound porches graced both the first and second floor.

This venture had been profitable. The plantation grew into its own small Cajun village here, just like they had back in

Acadia.

They had a shoemaker and a blacksmith. They made their own cooking vessels, dishes, and silverware. They had a mill to grind the grain into flour where it was baked into bread. They also made jellies and preserves. Living off of the land, they all shared the trials and tribulations of the times.

Marquette Plantation was the image of everything graceful and lovely in the Deep South. In the serene moonlight, ground fog swirled as a light breeze rolled off the bayou. Spanish moss dripped from the ancient oak trees, reminiscent of the lace curtains she had purchased.

She heard the moans of the poor lost souls trapped in the silver mist as it curled its way around the courtyard. The moon had a ring around it, promising rain soon. The misty halo created an eerie glow across the earth, bathing the area in a pale light.

Lately, she had been afraid to wander the grounds. The beauty of the night had been taken from her. All that remained in the place she loved for so long was death and evil. If only she knew where the evil lurked, she could warn someone. But she only sensed its presence, heard its raspy breath, and smelled the fetid odor that came from its flesh and blood.

She sat in the courtyard, looked toward the fields, and tried to see where this evil lurked tonight. The farmland was still just as rich and fertile. There were rows and rows of rice just starting to sprout up. She shook her head; no, it was no longer rice but sugarcane now.

How she missed when she could look out over the land and see its beauty, peace, and perfection. Lately, though, there was another presence, one that made her restless spirit uncomfortable. She saw the land drenched in blood. They had been fortunate during the war; their plantation had been spared. The silly soldiers had been easy to frighten off, but now would be different. Whatever had found a new life here was ugly and brutal, and she was unable to scare it off. The lost souls walked around aimlessly, crying out for help. She must try to find them, to learn what happened to them.

In her vision, she saw the area strewn with dead or dying women. They didn't speak; they only let out unearthly wails.

Genevieve never wanted for a thing, except not to die at such an early age. Her heart broke when Pierre married her younger sister so soon after her death. She tried to find reasoning behind his sudden marriage. She understood that he couldn't take care of their two rowdy sons and lively daughter without help, but he swore to love her until the end of time. Still, she had a hard time forgiving him for his marriage to Amanda, and now she forever wandered the plantation in hopes of finding him in death. She had yet to find him, and she no longer knew how long she had walked these grounds. Why did he move on without her? Did he not know she was bound to this earth in search of him?

Chapter 2
Marquette Plantation – Present Day

Walking outside, the morning sun greeted Bridgette. She usually loved the colorful sunrise, but not this morning. Today, she was heavy hearted. She never thought she would bury both of her parents at the same time, but as deep as their love was for each other, perhaps it was for the best. She heard that after a loved one passed away, the remaining spouse usually died soon after.

Tears filled Bridgette's eyes as she thought of her parents. She would never be able to forget that dreadful night; she came home to surprise them for the holidays only to come home to an empty house. Her parents had gone out to supper that night with some friends and on their way home an eighteen wheeler lost control of his load. She later learned that they died on impact.

As she drove into Rexma, she looked around and remembered what it had been like growing up here. Rexma was a somewhat rural Louisiana town along Bayou Renee. The Main Street ran right in the center of the town, with only one stop light. Tiny little stores lined the downtown, most of the businesses were family owned and operated. There was a barber shop, mechanic's shop, several restaurants, locksmith, a butcher and meat market that had all withstood the sands of time. Several specialty boutiques opened up here as well. Even the clothing shops, bookstores, and antique stores seemed to be flourishing. The closest chain store was about a half hour drive from here, and Bridgette didn't see one moving any closer, especially if the historical society had anything to say about it. At one time, Rexma had been a main hub on the bayou. Rice, sugarcane, cotton, and other agricultural products grown by local farmers for centuries were loaded on the barges and sent off to New Orleans.

This town was founded in 1763 and Bridgette's ancestors, the Marquette's, were among some of the first settlers here. Her family fled Acadia, now called Nova Scotia, and made their way down to Louisiana. Pierre Marquette knew how to farm the land and made his plantation a success; he had a green thumb and succeeded at whatever he did. From the research she'd done, her family never owned slaves; instead, they built a small Cajun community on the Marquette Plantation where they worked the land and kept to themselves. The plantation was self-contained, not wanting or needing help from the outside world.

Inside the funeral home, Bridgette greeted all of her parents' friends with a heavy heart. Marlys Landry came over and gave her a hug. "Mo chagren, I am so sorry pauvre ti bête. I still can't believe they are gone. If you need anything at all, call me. Your parents will be dearly missed."

She squeezed Mrs. Landry's hand, "Merci. You were such a good friend to Mom."

With tears in her eyes, Mrs. Landry said, "Mais, why is it that only the good die young?"

Bridgette saw Father Bill Rabelais enter the funeral home and walked over to him. She was ready to put this day behind her.

Father Rabelais walked over to the coffins and asked for everyone to join him in The Lord's Prayer. He performed a beautiful service full of respect for her parents. He read the standard funeral Bible verses and reminded all those attending that her parents were in a better place. At the end of the service he asked that everyone join in the Rosary.

When it was time to move her parents to their final resting place, Bridgette knew that not too many here would be joining them. Few would want to make the long three hour drive to New Orleans. Her parents had made all of their funeral arrangements not long after her dad had been diagnosed with Multiple Sclerosis. Her mom had been adamant that she did not want to be buried in the Marquette Family Cemetery located on the plantation grounds, but in her family's mausoleum in New Orleans. Her dad eventually agreed to her requests, as long as he could be buried near her.

Bridgette followed behind the hearse as the funeral procession meandered down the streets of New Orleans. As she drove through the wrought iron gates that separated the cemetery from the rest of New Orleans she noticed how exquisite their design was. Within this cemetery were buried some of the most famous, and infamous citizens, of New Orleans. Death played no favoritism. In the end, everyone was the same, ashes to ashes and dust to dust.

The family mausoleum was one of the older mausoleum's in the back of the cemetery. As they neared its location, she noticed that the manager of the cemetery was awaiting their arrival.

After parking her car, she watched as the coffins were wheeled out of the hearses and into the tiny room. Father Rabelais made his way to the front of the mausoleum, and waited to make sure that no other mourners would be joining them.

As Father Rabelias began to speak, his voice resonated in the small room. "Our Father, who art in heaven…"

The drive back to Marquette Plantation was a somber one. Childhood memories flashed through her mind as she made her way back to the plantation. It still amazed her at how time seemed to have stopped here in Rexma, Louisiana. Several houses and businesses kept their landmark status, preserving their history.

The sheer beauty of the drive did nothing to soothe her soul today. Right now, she craved the solitude of her new home to help console her. A white tail deer suddenly darted across the road, dashing into the foliage on the other side. She slowed down, in case he had a friend traveling with him, deer tended to run across the road here and drivers had to be careful.

Tomorrow morning she would begin making plans. She needed to explore the plantation to see if anything had to be renovated. The funeral had been lovely, but she was glad to be home and away from the dreariness that had hovered over her since their unexpected deaths.

The tires crunched as she drove over the white oyster shells that lined the circular driveway and she stopped in front of her family home. As she stepped out of her car, a cold breeze cut right through her. Even though Easter would be here soon, there was still a chill to the air. Spring was long overdue; she was ready for winter to come to an end.

Spring was supposed to be a time for new life to come into this world, not to be taken away. Yet here she was, coming back to an empty house after her parents' sudden demise. As you look up to the blue sky with pillows of motionless white clouds, you would think the weather outside was warm. When a sudden burst of cold air whipped across the horizon reminding you that winter has not let her grasp of the season go just yet.

She wished the skies were gray, and the weather thunderous to match her gloomy mood. She dreaded returning to an empty house and feared this day would never end. Would she ever come to terms with her parents' death? She would miss seeing her mother run out as soon as Bridgette drove up to greet her with warm kisses and asking about her day. No matter how bad her dad felt, he always had a sparkle in his eyes and a new joke to share with her. It is still such a terrible shock to her system that she lost not one, but both of her parents. If only she could kiss them each one more time, the tears built up inside of her once again as she realized she wouldn't be able to.

During the funeral, it had become hard to keep her erratic thoughts under control. The emotions of all her parents' friends and family began to close in and smother her. It took a great deal of strength on her part not to break down in tears in front of everyone. Throughout the day, she greeted guests from around the parish as they arrived to offer their condolences. Friends, several acquaintances, and what family they had remaining also stopped by. Bridgette vaguely remembered the conversations she had over the course of the day. She had more than likely repeated herself on more than one occasion.

She heard several of the rumors floating around town lately. Not too many people here had faith in her capabilities to keep this massive plantation afloat. Throughout the day, several people asked about her plans with regards to the plantation. Several land developers had been after her dad for years to sell them the property. Her roots were here, though, and she did not foresee selling for any amount of money.

She looked at her childhood home with a forlorn expression. She knew that someday it would be hers, but she never expected it to be this soon or under these circumstances.

As she moved closer to the front door, she noticed the mess. Her heart dropped as she saw someone had broken all the windows on the French doors that lined the front porch. Her resolve weakened as she looked at the disaster. Who would do such a thing, especially today of all days?

She searched through her purse for her phone to call Sheriff Jared Anslum. He would know who she could call to fix the broken windows.

"Sheriff Anslum this is Bridgette Marquette. I hate to bother you, but you did say if I need anything don't hesitate to call you. I just came back from the funeral and the front windows of the house are all broken."

Sheriff Anslum sighed into the phone, "Cher, mo chagren. I am so sorry to hear that. I will call Dwayne at Bayou Glass and have him go over there. Also, I will send Officer Graham Richard out to make a report."

She replied, "There is no reason to send an officer here, I just didn't know who to call to repair the damage."

"Mais non, I am going to send someone out there to check things out. Have you gone inside?"

"No, sir, I have not."

"Well, it would be best to let Officer Richard go in first, just in case."

She let out a sigh, "Mais oui. Yes, sir."

Bridgette couldn't get over the fact that someone did this to her house. As she was about to get back in her car to wait for Officer Richard, she heard car tires on the gravel driveway. Turning to see who it was, she let out an involuntary groan. She was in no mood to deal with him. The man might be able to turn a lady's head, but something about him made her uneasy.

He was worse than a thorn in her side. Not only did he pester her parents about selling, he hadn't let up with her. She watched as he stepped out of his brand new 2014 Mercedes SL500, being careful not to get dust on his Italian loafers. The man gave her the creeps, just being near him made her skin crawl.

"Ms. Marquette, I wanted to stop by and see how you are doing. I am sorry I didn't make it to your parents' funeral, but unfortunately I had some business that I needed to tend to."

Bridgette looked at the broken glass and wondered if he had something to do with this. She shook her head at the thought. He wouldn't get his hands dirty. Mais non, he was the type of person that paid someone to do his dirty work. Although, she could see him standing on the sidelines to make sure what he paid for gets done.

Bridgette took in his appearance and noticed as always, not a strand of hair was out of place. From the bronze color of his skin, she could tell he stayed in the tanning bed more than in the actual sun. When he smiled, his white teeth were in stark contrast to his skin. He not only dressed to perfection, but he had a physique that took hours spent in the gym to keep up. However, beneath the lovely exterior was pure ugliness on the inside. Bridgette looked Brett Gibson in the eyes, "Was there something I could do for you Mr. Gibson?"

Brett noted the disdain that dripped from her voice, "Now Ms. Marquette, that is no way to treat someone who came to offer their condolences for your loss."

"Mr. Gibson I know the real reason you are here, and it is not to offer your condolences. My answer will be the same as my dad's answer. I have no intentions of selling or leasing my land to you so that you can drill for oil. This land is too precious to me to have it destroyed by oil rigs."

He let out an exasperated sigh, "As I explained to your father, technology has come a long way in how we drill for oil. The land won't be destroyed; you can keep the house and open up your bed and breakfast, if that is what you want, and still allow us to drill for oil."

She shook her head, "No, my father was adamant about not leasing out or selling his land to the likes of you. He may be dead, but I intend to respect his wishes."

Brett Gibson stormed off to his car, slammed the door, and sped away. Officer Richard drove up while Brett drove off in a hurry and waited for the dust to settle before stepping out of his car.

Bridgette gave him a step by step account of what happened when she came home, also explaining how Mr. Gibson arrived just as she returned home.

Officer Richard asked, "Did he happen to ask about the broken glass?"

Bridgette shook her head, "Mais non, he never even brought it up."

Officer Richard scratched his head and looked at where the retreating car went down the drive. It was strange that he didn't ask about all the broken glass and offer to help. Unless, maybe you were the guilty party and wanted to judge that person's reaction to the destruction. He may need to talk with Mr. Gibson and find out what he was really doing here. Ms. Marquette wasn't the only one he had bothered lately. Several people had filed complaints with the Sheriff's Office regarding his strong-arm tactics.

***

From his rearview mirror, Brett Gibson watched as Bridgette talked to the young police officer. What were they talking about? Had she somehow figured out what he had been up to behind her back?

He shook his head. No, he had been careful in hiding his tracks. She couldn't possibly know, could she? Still, he would keep a close eye on her.

***

Once Bridgette was finally alone in the house, she walked into her bedroom and plopped down on her bed. After a few minutes, she pulled herself up and walked into the bathroom. She looked at her reflection in the mirror. The stress and fatigue of the day showed on her face. Despite her resolution to stay strong, the grief over the loss of her parents became too much. Crumpling to the bathroom floor, she gave in to the tears. She allowed the tears and grief to wash over her. She felt so helpless and alone. As she sat there crying, a calming presence came over her, and she swore she felt arms wrap around her. After the last of the tears flowed, she started the shower and prepared for bed. Tomorrow was another day, and she had a lot to do if she wanted to open a bed and breakfast soon.

Marquette Plantation had remained a grand plantation. Back in the day, there were no other plantations near that could equal its grandeur or its farm production. It only needed a little tender loving care to bring it back to its original grandeur again. Her family home was a sight that took your breath away, just looking at it inspired awe in her.

It sat at the end of a long, curvy drive flanked on both sides with ancient oak trees dripping with Spanish moss. The front of the house had three sets of French doors that graced the front porch. Setting off each set of French doors were louvered shutters painted rich ebony black. A horseshoe shaped double stairway graced the entrance way. When the hardwood floors were sanded down and refinished, it would be breathtaking. The enormity of the house took her breath away when she thought of all she still had to do. There were close to thirty rooms that had to be tended to before she could even begin to think of opening her bed and breakfast. On the second floor, there were over fifteen rooms she could rent out. There was also a coach house, a stable and the old blacksmith shop that were all still well preserved. Her family took great pride in making sure over the years nothing fell to neglect. She planned on eventually hiring someone to help with tours at the plantation. She wanted to keep the memories of this place alive for years to come. There were a few bed and breakfasts in the area, but none offered an authentic experience of living on a plantation.

Bridgette had already spoken to several people who were willing to help with the tours for a small salary along with room and board. Each of the out buildings still had rooms attached, but they needed to be brought up to more modern standards before she offered room and board.

She was even considering the addition of a glass blowing

shop here at the plantation. That should bring in the crowds, especially if they sold items made on the plantation.

There was also an old cabin that was used for bootlegging moonshine on the property years ago. Eventually, she wanted to restore it fully. It was nestled in a corner away from the main house, almost hidden in the swamp. It was in its own little world back there; framed by several large magnolia, cypress, and ancient oak trees shrouded with Spanish moss. Her great, great grand-pere was known as one of the most notorious bootleggers in the parish.

Several silos on the property had to be checked out structurally. When her ancestors began to farm the land, they chose to plant rice and soybeans. Some years, an increase in profits helped them through the tight times. Sugarcane farming did not start here until much later.

Back when the plantation first began, the steamboats traveled along the bayou selling mercantile, as well as picking up the goods to bring up and down the river system. Back then, they even had to wait for the priest to come via boat to perform wedding and baptism ceremonies. The old pier was still in good condition and could be used to fish on or to enjoy the scenery.

Available in eBook and Paperback